Mill

by rising star

Jennifer Taylor

We hope you'll enjoy this wonderfully emotional novella—in which working together day and night leads to an unexpected proposition, on the most romantic of all days... *Valentine's Day*!

Michael Callan met Claire Parkinson three years ago, but now fate's conspired to throw them back together. It's only a matter of time before they give in to temptation!

Turn the pages to discover whether Claire will agree to a very enticing proposal...

Jennifer Taylor was born in Liverpool, England, and still lives in the north-west, several miles outside the city. Books have always been a passion of hers, so it seemed natural to choose a career in librarianship, a wise decision as the library is where she met her husband, Bill. Twenty years and two children later, they are still happily married, with the added bonus that she has discovered how challenging and enjoyable writing romantic fiction can be!

PRAISE FOR THE AUTHOR

Jennifer Taylor has written over twenty books for Tender Romance™. She's also written more than fifteen books for our exciting Medical Romance™ series and is now focusing all her talents into writing intense, heartwarming medical dramas.

Don't miss Jennifer's next sensational Medical Romance™, an emotional emergency set in a bustling A&E department!

Look out for
***Life Support* by Jennifer Taylor**

Senior Registrar Michelle Roberts enjoys working in St Justin's Emergency department. It provides all the drama she needs! But Dominic Walsh's arrival makes her confront her emotions, and suddenly accepting all the love and support she's been missing becomes Michelle's number one priority.

On sale May 2002, in Medical Romance™

All the characters in this book have no existence outside the imagination of the author, and have no relation whatsoever to anyone bearing the same name or names. They are not even distantly inspired by any individual known or unknown to the author, and all the incidents are pure invention.

First published in Great Britain 1993
Harlequin Mills & Boon Limited,
Eton House, 18-24 Paradise Road, Richmond, Surrey, TW9 1SR

ISBN 0 263 83196 5

54-0102

Printed and bound in Spain
by Litografia Rosés S.A., Barcelona

Violets are Blue

Jennifer Taylor

MILLS & BOON®

CHAPTER ONE

HE HADN'T changed. Oh, there were traces of silver in the black hair at his temples, a few more lines around those light green eyes which made such a startling contrast to the darkness of his tanned skin, but basically he hadn't changed.

Michael Callan had walked out of that very door almost three years before but as he stood there now, tall and arrogant, staring around the assembled group, Claire experienced again that familiar, disturbing surge of awareness—only this time she ruthlessly suppressed it. He might not have changed, but she had! She was no longer the foolish, trusting girl who had worn her heart on her sleeve. This time her relationship with Michael Callan was going to be strictly business!

'Cal! Good to see you. How was the flight?' Tom Jackson, manager of the store, hurried forwards, a beaming smile barely concealing the anxiety they all shared. Michael Callan had built himself the reputation of a hard taskmaster in the past few years and he wouldn't be pleased about recent events. The fact that he had come himself from New York to sort out the problems at Hadley's London store, flagship of the worldwide chain his family had built its fortune on, was proof of that.

'Tom.' He shook the man's hand then walked past him to take the seat behind the desk as though it was his right, and Claire felt her blood start to boil at the deliberate slight to Tom. Without a word she got up and fetched another chair, setting it next to hers in the row lined up in front of the huge mahogany desk.

Thanks.' Tom sat down and smiled nervously around the room at the rest of the staff, who were starting to look uneasy. 'I think you know everyone here, don't you, Cal? I'd just like to say on behalf of us all what a pleasure it is——'

'Let's cut the formalities, shall we, Tom, and get right down to business?' Cal opened the case he'd set on top of the desk and drew out a folder before glancing along the row. Claire steeled herself for that moment when his eyes would meet hers, for that first hint of recognition, but he did no more than skim a cool glance over her face before his gaze travelled on. 'You all know why I am here. What I want to hear now is an explanation as to why this branch is losing money. We are at present in the position of making a loss of some seventeen per cent each month. That is totally unacceptable and unless we can find some way to reverse the situation fast then I'm afraid this store will have to close.'

'Close? But Cal, you can't really mean that. . .?' Tom tailed off, looking helplessly around at all the other stunned faces.

'I rarely say things I don't mean. Right, I asked that you should all prepare a report on the state of your departments, outlining your plans for the future. Let's start with you, shall we, Graham? Electrical is just about holding its own thanks to the Christmas trade but it still isn't doing the sort of turnover we expect. Let's hear your views.'

He sat back in the leather swivel chair, loosening his

tie and unbuttoning the collar of his white shirt in a gesture that was achingly familiar to Claire. He had always hated the restriction of formal clothing, pulling off his tie and unbuttoning the collar of his shirt as soon as he'd got home to the flat they had shared so briefly. So many memories, so many fragments of a past they had once shared, all the love, all the laughter, held at bay these past years, yet suddenly they came rushing back and the room and the steady drone of Graham's voice faded.

'Claire!' She jumped when Tom dug her hard in the ribs, colouring as she caught sight of all the faces turned her way.

'Sorry,' she said quickly. 'I missed that.'

'I asked if you would like to give your report next, Claire. If it isn't too much trouble, that is.'

The sarcasm in his deep voice stung. Claire lifted her head, meeting the frosty green stare across the desk with an equally cool one of her own. 'Of course, Mr Callan.'

His jaw tightened at the deliberate, mocking formality, his hand contracting around the folder of notes, and just for a second Claire regretted what she'd said, before tossing the silky blonde bob of hair back from her flushed face in a gesture of defiance. It was about time that someone pricked that damnable composure of his! He'd got too used to being the one to cut people down, but, still, it wouldn't be wise to antagonise him too much.

Conscious of the icy atmosphere, she gave her report, keeping her eyes centred on her notes until she came to the end. 'In the absence of Miss Jones, our departmental head, I didn't feel it appropriate that I should put forward any plans for the future. I am sure that she must have her own ideas and would prefer to discuss them with you herself.'

'Perhaps she would; however, as Miss Jones is absent yet again through sickness, that isn't possible. The directive I issued was quite straightforward, Claire. I asked that each and every department head or his assistant should prepare a report stating why turnover is down and what improvements can be made in the future.' He glanced down at the notes he'd spread on the desk, his face uncompromising as he looked back at her. 'Over recent months Greetings Cards and Gifts is one of the departments that has shown the greatest losses. So may I suggest that you take yourself into the outer office and start putting a few ideas down on paper—that is if you can manage to keep your mind fully on the business at hand? Now, David, how about——?'

'Just a minute! Who do you think you are to speak to me like that? I am not some schoolgirl whom you can tell off for not doing her homework! I didn't outline any plans for the department because I felt it wasn't my place to do so!' She was so angry that she could hardly see straight, lights flashing across her blurred vision. How she loathed him! Loathed him for his arrogance, his cold, unremitting use of authority, his total lack of any human feelings. He had always had a tendency towards high-handedness when they had lived together and she had foolishly gone along with it, too blinded by her love for him to want to argue. He had meant everything to her then. She had lived just to hear him laugh, to see him smile at her as though she was someone special in his life, but no more. She'd had a cruel awakening to the fact that it had all been a lie. He had taken what he'd wanted from her then tossed her aside, too intent on pursuing his own driving ambitions to care about her.

'No, you aren't a schoolgirl, Claire, even though it appears you intend to act like one. You are an employee of this company. . .remember?' He sat back, flexing his shoulders as though he was tired, but there was no weariness about the grim set of his face as he stared at her then looked around at the rest of the group. 'I want to make one thing clear here and now to everyone in this room and that is that I am not interested in hurt pride, injured feelings or any other such emotions. All I'm concerned about is getting this store back on its feet, or, if that proves impossible, in closing it down while causing the least damage possible to the rest of the chain.' He studied each person in turn before his gaze returned to Claire's flushed face. 'If that causes a problem for any one of you then I expect you to tell me now.'

'I'm sure we are all with you on this, Cal.' Tom broke the tense silence that had fallen over the room. 'We are all committed to bringing the London branch back to the top of the league.'

'That's all I wanted to hear.' He turned away, ignoring Claire, who quietly gathered up her notes and left the room. She closed the door, shutting out the sound of his deep voice, wishing it were as easy to shut him completely out of her mind. She'd been dreading their meeting ever since she'd heard that he was coming back, but nothing could have prepared her for that confrontation.

She went and sat down at the desk, spreading her

notes in front of her, but her mind was far away. All she could think of was Cal's voice, so cold and impersonal as he'd reminded her that she was an employee. She had to remember that that was all she was to him now and lock the memories of those golden days when they had loved and laughed together deep in the back of her mind. It was over and they'd both moved on; she'd rebuilt her life, made new friends, and she wouldn't allow any feelings of bitterness to destroy all that she'd worked so hard to achieve. She was an employee, and that suited her just fine!

With a sigh, she forced herself to concentrate on drawing up the plans he wanted. Not that it was a difficult task. She had plenty of ideas, most of them firmly squashed by Miss Jones at one time or another. The elderly head of department had her own fixed ideas on how things should be run, and didn't welcome interference. Now, however, Claire allowed her imagination free rein.

When the connecting door between the offices opened, she didn't glance up, assuming that Tom had been sent to fetch her back into the meeting. 'Just give me a second. I'd better make sure that our dear boss has everything he wants otherwise I shall be well and truly in the doghouse——' She broke off, horrified to see Cal when she finally glanced around. 'I. . .I didn't realise it was you. I thought it was Tom.'

'Obviously. How are you getting along? Have you managed to put some ideas down on paper?' The cool, dismissive note in his voice hurt. This man had held her, kissed her, made love to her, yet now he spoke to her as though she were a stranger!

She stood up, tidying the papers into a pile, her blue

eyes bright as glass as they met his. 'I have plenty of ideas. Did you think I hadn't? Were you using this as some sort of test to see if I can cope?' She shook her head, the silky pale hair swinging back and forth. 'Sorry to disappoint you, Mr Callan, but I am not lacking in ability to do my job!'

'I never imagined that you were. You wouldn't be working here if that was the case. I have kept track of your progress, Claire, and I have to admit that I've been impressed with your achievements so far. You've gone from a junior sales position to assistant departmental head in less than three years. That proves that you have the ability as long as you don't allow personal feelings to interfere.'

He turned to go but Claire caught his arm, her fingers closing around the hard muscles under the smooth, fine wool of his grey suit. 'And that isn't something anyone can ever accuse you of doing, is it, Cal? You never allow personal feelings to interfere in business.' She laughed, a hollow sound that held a note of scorn. 'Don't I know that! You were quite happy to use me for your own ends while you were maintaining that masquerade of being just an ordinary employee but once you'd assumed your rightful position as one of the Hadley family then you couldn't wait to get rid of me, could you? You didn't want me then.'

'That's where you're wrong.' With a speed that was alarming, he swung her round and caught her hand as she tried to draw it away from his arm. 'I wanted you a lot, sweet, seductive little Claire.' He pulled her closer, his fingers hard around hers. 'I could still want you now, in fact. Is that what this is all about? Is that why you're trying to provoke my anger—to see if there is still that same marvellous sexual chemistry between us?' He hauled her to him, his arms closing around her body. 'Let's test it out, shall we?'

'No! Cal, stop it! Stop——!' His mouth closed over hers, his lips bruising as he kissed her with a deliberate passion. Claire tried to turn her head away to escape the kiss, but his finger burrowed under her long, pale hair, forcing her to stay where she was. She moaned softly, hating the rough assault of his mouth on hers, and felt him still for a moment before slowly the bruising pressure eased and he began to kiss her in a way that sent a sudden fierce sensation of heat along her veins. This time his lips weren't trying to punish —they were seducing, warm and mobile, awakening memories of other times when he had kissed her just this way. Time seemed to be suspended, the past rolling into the present, then Cal put her from him and everything shot back into bitter, sharp focus.

'So now we know the spark is still there if and when we ever choose to rekindle it. But I'm afraid we shall have to leave any further discussions, tempting though they may be, until later. There are more pressing matters to attend to now.'

'There won't be any later!' She rubbed her mouth, feeling shaken to the core by what had happened. She'd convinced herself that she was over him, but how could she be when one deliberate kiss could light this fire inside her again?

'Oh, I think there will. There has to be, and you know that, Claire. However, everyone is waiting for your report right now.'

He went back through to the inner office, leaving the door open for her to follow. Claire took a shaky breath then smoothed her ruffled hair back from her hot face. How she hated him, now more than ever! She would cling to that thought to get through the rest of the day. After all, in a few hours' time he would be back in New York and that would be the end of it all.

She was aware of the speculative looks cast her way as she walked back into the meeting but she ignored them, focusing all her attention on Cal, unwilling to give him the chance to take her to task again after the last disturbing occasion.

'Right, then, Claire, let's hear your plans.' He looked down at his notes to check some figures, his tone cool and quite impersonal once more. 'Greetings Cards has been steadily declining for some time now, apart from a small upsurge at Christmas. So what do you propose to do to rectify the situation?'

Claire glanced at what she'd written, hesitant now about putting her ideas forward, but that upsurge in business he'd mentioned had been the result of her planning when Miss Jones had first gone off sick. Maybe she wasn't so way off track after all. 'It seems to me that the real problem lies in the fact that there has always been a tendency to let greetings cards sell themselves. People need a card for birthdays, Christmas and so on. There's never been much promotional work done in the past.' She paused for a moment, but Cal's face was totally impassive so she hurried on. 'It will be cutting things fine as we're already into January but I would like to do a big promotion centred around St Valentine's Day. Oh, I know we always do a display of the cards, but I want to do more than that. I want to really push the idea of sending a valentine this year, make the public feel that it is something they *must* do.'

'And how do you intend to do that?' Cal straightened, his eyes narrowing on her with interest in their green depths. How she'd used to love looking into those eyes, used to thrill at the way the colour would change from palest clear green to a stormy jade as he'd been aroused to passion. Now just the memory was enough to make her breathless so that it was an effort to remember where she was and what had just happened between them. She was more vulnerable around Cal than she cared to admit.

'I was hoping that we could run some sort of a competition as a draw, perhaps offer a weekend in Paris for the winner, with champagne for the runners-up. The whole store can be involved even if it's just by carrying the entry forms, but we could decorate selected departments with hearts, flowers and devote window space to the theme. Fashion, lingerie, the flowershop, all can contribute something, I'm sure, but obviously Greeting Cards will be the central point of the promotion, offering a gift-wrap service, balloons, maybe even handwritten valentines. We could hope to increase turnover by around fifty per cent during the weeks running up to Valentine's Day itself.'

'I see. Interesting.' He tapped his fingers on the desk. 'We've had Christmas, we're in the middle of the sales, so it would mean a lot of hard work for everyone.'

'I'm sure none of us would mind that, Cal.' Tom leant forwards, an earnest expression on his pleasant face. 'We are all very anxious about the store's future and not just because of our jobs. This shop is an institution: it would be a crying shame to see it forced to close. We want it back at the top!'

'And this along with the rest of the ideas you've all put forward today could help achieve that. Good. That's what I wanted to hear. I had reservations when I came over on the plane as to whether the commitment was still as strong as it used to be, but obviously it is. If we work together then I'm sure we can keep this store open.'

There was a collective sigh of relief as he stopped speaking. Cal smiled suddenly, looking so much more like the man she had once fallen in love with that Claire felt her heart start to ache. How different would her life have been if Cal had been what she'd thought he was—a young man working his way to the top? She had no idea, just the cold certainty of knowing that it was pointless to speculate now.

'I can see you're all relieved. I know it hasn't been easy for any of you recently. My uncle was unwell for some time before he retired and didn't keep the control he should have done over the business. However, that is in the past. Now I have a few suggestions I want to put to you—nothing earth-shattering, mind, just a few ideas to prove that I am prepared to do my share of the work.' He looked round, his gaze lingering almost deliberately on Claire so that she had the strangest feeling that he knew she wasn't going to like what he was about to say.

'The American end of the business is very healthy at present. So much so that I feel I can safely leave it in other capable hands while I come back to England and concentrate on getting this branch back up to standard. I won't be usurping Tom's position as manager. I shall be working in an advisory capacity with each department in turn and in view of what I've just heard I propose that the first department I shall turn my attention on is Greetings Cards and Gifts. Claire and I shall be working together on the valentine project.'

Proposal? That wasn't a proposal! The word proposal implied a degree of flexibility, a chance to consider the facts and *then* make a decision. This was all cut and dried. Michael Callan was coming back to England to work in the store. . .to work with *her*. . .and there wasn't a thing she could do or say to make him change his mind!

CHAPTER TWO

'I'D LIKE a word with you before you go, Claire.'

Claire glanced after the rest of the group, a trace of desperation in her eyes as Tom closed the door to leave her and Cal alone in the office. 'I really have to get back. What do you want?'

He glanced at his watch then slipped the folder into the case as he came round the desk. 'Just a few words in private. I have to catch the afternoon flight back to New York but I have a couple of hours before I need to be at the airport. We may as well have some lunch.'

'I don't want any lunch, thank you. Look, Cal, I have nothing whatsoever to say to you of a private nature. Now, if you'll excuse me, I must go. We're short-staffed with Miss Jones being off.'

'And that's what I want to talk to you about.' He steered her out of the office and along the corridor to the lift before she had time to draw breath to object again. 'Sorry if I made it sound as though I had something personal to say to you. It's purely business, I can assure you, but something I don't want spreading around until all the details are finalised.'

He summoned the lift, raising a quizzical brow when she hovered uncertainly at his side, not sure if she should believe him or not. 'Scout's honour, Claire. This is business. And don't go worrying about the department. I had a word with Tom earlier and he's arranged cover over the lunchtime period.'

'I doubt very much if you were ever a Scout and as for honour...!' She smiled waspishly at him. 'I don't think you have much idea what that word means.'

He laughed slowly, standing aside for her to precede him into the lift. 'What a little firebrand you've turned into, Claire. You used to be a whole lot more amenable three years ago.'

'I was a lot of things three years ago, but I've grown up now, Cal. I'm not some gullible young girl now!'

'No, you're not.' He slid a gaze over her, his eyes lingering on her slender figure in a way that sent heat rushing along her veins. 'You're how old now—twenty-three...four? And a very beautiful woman who obviously knows what she wants from life and intends to have it. Yes, Claire, you have changed.'

'Well, you haven't! You always were arrogant and self-opinionated. It may surprise you to learn that I don't give a toss what you think of me now!'

'No?' He studied her flushed face in silence, then let his eyes meet hers and linger for a heartbeat. 'Then why are you getting so upset?'

'I am not getting upset!' She drew in a deep breath, forcing the anger down, willing herself to stay calm. 'Look, Cal, this is ridiculous. We are two adults who once shared...well, shared a relationship, but it's all in the past and I'd be grateful if you wouldn't keep on trying to remind me of it all the time. Frankly, it isn't something I want to remember all that much!'

'Yet you were the one who started it this morning at the meeting. Be honest with yourself, Claire, and admit that you would never have dreamt of challenging me that way if we hadn't shared that...relationship.'

His eyes bored into hers, brilliant green, searching...

for what? An admission that he was right? They both knew that he was. 'No, I wouldn't, but nor would you have spoken to me in that tone either, Michael Callan. You want honesty, do you? Well, then, I'll be honest and tell you straight that the thought of having to work with you for the next few weeks isn't pleasant!'

'Why not? Surely you've worked with other men you've dated? You aren't trying to tell me that you've led the life of a nun for almost three years, or that all the men in the store are blind to your obvious attractions?' His tone was mocking, bringing a flush of colour to her face. When the lift stopped at the ground floor she could hardly wait to get out, hurrying ahead of him towards the taxi he pointed out that was waiting in the car park, using the few minutes it took to get in to gather her composure around her.

Yes, she had dated several of the men who worked at the store, and was still on friendly terms with them, but then none had touched her emotions as Cal had done. He had been the yardstick she had unconsciously measured them against and each one had fallen short. It was easy to work with them now, but it wouldn't be easy to work with Cal and that bothered her. If she were really over him then it shouldn't have mattered, should it?

The thought held her silent on the short drive to the small, exclusive restaurant down by the river. Claire stepped out on to the pavement, jumping nervously when Cal slid a hand under her elbow to guide her in through the door. She moved away from him, looking round the room, studying the subdued lighting, the crisp white tablecloths, the clientele whose very appearance spoke of wealth, then turned to smile coldly at Cal.

'Showing your true colours now, I see.' She indicated the subtle opulence of the restaurant with a dismissive sweep of her hand, icy scorn ringing in her voice. 'I don't recall us visiting places like this before, but then, of course, you were keeping up that pretence of being just another Hadley employee.'

His brows lowered, his face grim and remote as he studied her in silence for a moment. 'And I don't recall us *wanting* to come to places like this. We were happy with the simple things in life, remember? However, I brought you here today not to impress upon you how things have changed but to reassure you. I use this place for business whenever I'm in town.'

As though to emphasise the point the head waiter came over, greeting Cal by name as he led them to a table in the far corner of the room. Claire sat down, smoothing the linen napkin across her knees, wishing she'd held her tongue. She *did* remember how things had been, how a simple picnic in the park had meant more than any expensive gourmet meal. The magical ingredient had been love and that had turned even the most ordinary outing into something special.

'You never did answer my question.' His voice drew her out of her reverie. Claire sat up straighter, forcing herself to meet his eyes across the table and ignore the echoes of the past.

'What question?'

'About who you've dated in the store.' He put the menu down, leaning back in the gilt-framed chair, his expression both cool and mocking, instantly kindling her temper again.

'I don't see that it's any of your business, do you?'

'Maybe not, but I can't help but be curious as to what you've been doing since we broke up.'

'Well, I haven't been sitting around pining for you!' she snapped.

'I never imagined that you would have. So come on, then, Claire, tell me who the man in your life is at present. Is it anyone from the store or someone with no connections there at all?'

What should she say? How could she admit that there was no one special in her life and hadn't been since he'd left? That was the one thing she had no intention of admitting!

'Not that I see what business it is of yours, but Tom and I have been seeing each other recently.' It was such a small lie but she crossed her fingers anyway as she uttered it. She had been out with Tom on several occasions but both had soon realised that the relationship would go no further than friendship.

'Tom? Now that does surprise me.' He steepled his fingers, staring at her over the top in a way that made her want to wriggle in the seat, but she curbed the urge.

'Yes! We enjoy each other's company. Is that a crime?'

He ignored the sarcasm, smiling calmly back at her. 'No. Tom is a nice enough guy but he's hardly your type, Claire.'

'Is that right? And what makes you such an expert on the type of man I need?' She let her eyes drift over him, clasping her hands tightly together on the napkin, afraid that she would be sorely tempted to reach over and slap his arrogant face. 'I don't really think that you have any idea of my taste in men.'

'Haven't I indeed?' He leant forwards suddenly, pinning her with a glance. 'Let's not play games, Claire. We both know the type of man you need.'

'Meaning you, I suppose?' Sensations were rushing through her, threatening to destroy her composure, but she fought against them with a steely determination that stemmed from fear of letting him see how she really felt. 'Sorry, Cal, but I think not. A few years ago maybe, but now the type of man who attracts me isn't the least like you. He's warm, caring, a man who puts relationships before the demands of business.' She smiled bitterly back at him, feeling her heart aching with a sharp, fresh pain. 'I'm afraid that you don't fit that bill at all.'

'No?' He reached out and caught her chin, smoothing the pad of his thumb across her mouth, watching the way her lips parted almost helplessly under the evocative caress. 'I'm sure I could make you change your mind about that.'

'I. . .' It was hard to think while he was touching her like this but she had to try, had to break this spell he was casting over her again. She jerked her head away, running her hand across her mouth to wipe away the lingering sensation of heat. 'I don't want you to change my mind. I'm perfectly happy with my life the way it is. Now I believe that you said you had something you wanted to discuss with me, something to do with work, that is?'

It was an effort to keep her voice level but she managed it. She couldn't afford to let him see how shaken she felt. It would give him an advantage she couldn't afford to lose. Michael Callan was a worthy opponent no matter what game he chose to play. Why he should choose to play this one now was beyond her but she had to keep her head and remember how dangerous he could be.

He sat back, smiling faintly as he studied the warmth in her smooth cheeks. 'I shall have to take your word for it that you are happy, then, Claire, but I have my doubts. However, now isn't the time to debate the point. . .not in such a public place, at least——' He broke off as the waiter came to take their order. Claire opted for the chef's salad, knowing she couldn't manage anything more substantial. Her stomach was a churning mass of nerves thanks to Cal. She had no intention of letting him walk all over her but it would be foolish to start an argument. She had to stay calm and let him believe that she didn't care what he thought. After all it wasn't a lie: she *did* like her life the way it was now, neat and ordered, uncluttered by any deep emotional entanglements. If she occasionally yearned for the excitement and passion that had been such an integral part of their relationship then she had learned to keep such feelings locked at the very back of her mind.

'Right, we'd better get down to business, then.' Cal glanced at his watch then back at her, his expression coolly impersonal once more. 'Over the past few months I have become increasingly concerned about Miss Jones's frequent absences. It is a situation that I feel cannot be allowed to continue.'

'What do you mean?' Claire stared back at him in consternation. 'I know she's been sick a lot recently but surely you can't be planning on dismissing her?

She's been with the firm over thirty years! That should count for something even with you!'

His mouth thinned with displeasure. 'I am well aware of how long she has worked for us, and *no*, I am not planning on dismissing her. I have a very strong sense of loyalty towards Hadley's employees, especially those who have given the sort of devotion to the company that Miss Jones has.'

Claire had the grace to blush at the rebuke but she wouldn't apologise for what she'd said until he'd made it clear what he intended. 'Then what are you planning on doing about it?'

'I have already started the ball rolling. I asked Tom to visit her at home and find out if she would be interested in taking early retirement.' He shrugged. 'It's a benefit I've been keen to introduce for some time and now seems like the ideal opportunity.'

'I see, and what did she say about the idea?'

'Once she discovered that financially she would lose very little, she was delighted to accept. It seems that work has become increasingly stressful for her of late and I think she was just relieved to discover that she could retire earlier than she'd planned.'

His consideration shouldn't have surprised her. The Cal she remembered had always been a caring man who had willingly helped others less able than himself. Yet somehow over the years they'd been apart she'd built up this picture in her mind of a cold, ruthless despot, storing the rumours about his tough business deals as evidence of the fact. Had it been a deliberate attempt on her part to find things to dislike about him? She had the uncomfortable and disturbing feeling it had.

Guilt made her smile warmly at him. 'I think it's a marvellous idea. I know she finds it hard to cope but she's just tried to carry on.'

'Well, this should solve her problems and ours as well. We need people in this store who are open to fresh ideas, Claire. Staff who aren't so deeply rooted in traditions that they won't try something different. With that in mind I have decided to offer you the position of head of department when Miss Jones leaves. What do you say?'

'Me? I. . . Well. . . Why me, Cal?' She shook her head, trying to clear the jumble of thoughts, and felt a cold wave of sickness envelop her as a sudden unpalatable thought struck her. 'There are many others who have worked for the firm longer than I have and who are better qualified to take over the job, so why offer it to me? It isn't meant to be some sort of a sweetener, is it?'

His eyes narrowed at the sharpness of her tone but he spoke calmly. 'No, it isn't. What a suspicious little mind you have, Claire.'

'Is it any wonder?' She drew in a slow breath but it was hard to stay unemotional. 'I've not had much reason to trust you, Cal, so is it any wonder if I view this offer with more than a trace of scepticism?'

'This is business, Claire. You above anyone should know that I never put personal feelings before business decisions. His eyes held hers, cold, glacial, so remote that she felt a sharp stab of pain and wished for a moment that she hadn't voiced her concerns before she realised that she was doing it again, allowing him to manipulate her emotions. She couldn't afford to soften.

She had to find out exactly what was behind this offer of promotion.

'I still don't accept that I'm the best person for the job, not because I don't feel that I can cope with it but because of the mere fact that I have only been assistant departmental head for less than a year. There are others who've been waiting for promotion far longer than that.'

'There are, but that doesn't mean that they are ready to handle it. As far as I'm concerned, Claire, you are the one person who can put that department back on its feet. The ideas that you outlined this morning only serve to emphasise that. All I want to know is if you are willing to accept.'

'I. . .' What should she say? It was a golden opportunity, something she'd been working towards, but could she trust him? Yet on the other hand why should she throw all her hard work away? As he'd just said, she knew that business always came first in his life.

'Come on, Claire. What's the problem? Yes or no?' There was mockery in his deep voice and she glared at him. He was the problem and he knew it! Knew that her reluctance stemmed from a fear of being drawn back into his life. But she was her own woman now: he couldn't make her do anything that she didn't want to. The days when she had hung on to Michael Callan's every word and rushed to fulfil his every whim were long past!

'Yes. Thank you, I shall accept.'

'Good. I was hoping that you would.' He smiled at her, his eyes so warm that a shiver raced down her spine. He picked up the bottle of wine and filled their glasses, then raised his in a toast. 'Here's to us, Claire. To our new. . .alliance.'

Claire picked up her glass, her hand trembling as she touched it lightly against his then set it down again. Had she done the right thing? Or had she just made the biggest mistake of her life? She had the uncomfortable feeling that only time would tell.

'There's a few phone calls I need to make. I'll be upstairs if you need me, Claire. Just phone through. Oh, and leave the rest of that display until I get back.'

Claire stiffened at the sound of the slow, deep voice. She should have become used to having Cal around by now but she hadn't. He'd been working in the department for over a week yet she still hadn't found a way to quell this instant surge of awareness every time he spoke. She glanced over her shoulder to where he stood, immaculate in a dark grey suit and pale blue shirt that did all the right things for his tall, leanly muscled body, and sighed. Why did he have to come back?

'All right? Can you manage, then?'

Did he *mean* to make it sound as though she couldn't? Claire didn't bother giving him the benefit of the doubt as she stared coldly back. 'I shall try my best, but don't worry, Mr Callan, I shall phone you up if I find that I can't!'

His face tightened, his green eyes frosty. 'Feel free.' He turned away, walking briskly towards the escalator without a backward glance. Claire watched him go, ruing the fact that she had let her temper get the better of her again. It had kept happening all the time this past week and it was starting to worry her. She wasn't normally so quick-tempered, but there again the situation wasn't exactly normal, was it?

Annoyed with both herself and him, she glanced round at the silk hearts and gilt cupids that decorated the department. Everyone had worked so hard getting the promotion off the ground and it was nearly finished, just another few items to be set in place. She'd be damned if she'd stand about wasting time until Cal chose to come back. She would finish it off herself.

Hadley's was an old building, with elegant wooden panelling stretching up to high ornate ceilings, but it was only when she reached the top of the ladder that Claire fully realised just how high they were. She stopped to catch her breath then reached over to hang the last gilt cupid into place, gasping when the ladder slipped a fraction so that she was forced to grab hold of the cupid to steady herself, then found to her horror that she couldn't seem to persuade herself to let it go again. She seemed to be frozen in place, one hand clutching the shiny gilt cupid, the other clinging to the ladder.

'Claire! What the hell are you doing? Get down at once!' There was no mistaking the anger in Cal's voice but she found it as impossible to answer as she did to move. Grimly, she hung on then gave a tiny scream when the ladder shook.

'It's all right. I'm just coming up there to get you.' His voice was soft, soothing; it seemed to break the spell and she looked round, eyes widening when she saw him climbing up to stand just beneath her.

'Now I want you to move your foot slowly down to the next rung. Can you do that for me, Claire?'

'Y-yes.' She inched her foot off the tread to feel for

the one below. Cal's fingers closed gently around her ankle, warm and firmly reassuring as he positioned her foot in place.

'Good. And again, just another step. Slowly now. There's no need to rush.' His fingers brushed the back of her leg as he moved down a rung and prepared to help her again and Claire shuddered, finding far more danger in that disturbing touch than in being stuck twenty feet off the ground!

'I can manage now. You don't need to help me any more,' she said faintly.

'I'm sure you can but let's do this my way.' Once again his fingers found the slim curve of her ankle, then slid up her calf to steady her as she stepped down. Claire bit her lip, feeling shivers of fire fanning out from where his hand rested on her leg. Without another word she let him help her, gasping when he lifted her the last few feet then slowly let her slide to the ground. She moved away from him at once, conscious of the fact that her pulse was racing, and not just from fear. What was it about him that affected her so? She wished she knew, then maybe she could find some way to cure this awareness she always felt when he was near.

'Thank you,' she said stiffly. 'But I could have managed.'

'Could you indeed? It didn't look that way to me! What a stupid thing to do. What were you trying to prove, Claire? Just how well you can do everything by yourself? Well, I'm afraid it misfired this time, my sweet!'

'Don't you "my sweet" me! And I wasn't trying to prove anything. I just wanted to get the display finished.'

'And that was more important than your safety?'

'Of course not! I was perfectly safe. It just startled me when the ladder slipped but I could have got down without your help.'

'Oh, come on!' He shook his head, a lock of dark hair falling rakishly across his brow when she started to protest. 'Save your breath. We both know that you were too scared to move. It was pure stubbornness that made you climb up there in the first place instead of waiting for me to do it.'

'I *could* have got down! However, if you choose to see yourself as my rescuer, then feel free. As for my being stubborn, well, I have no idea why you should think that.' She went to walk away, incensed by his high-handedness and his perceptive reading of the situation, but he caught her arm and stopped her, an expression on his face that sent an immediate *frisson* down her spine.

'You seem to forget how well I know you, Claire.' His hand slid down her arm, his fingers burning through the thin silk of her white blouse as they laced around her wrist. 'I remember just how stubborn you can be at times.'

'So what do you expect me to say? Should I feel flattered that you remember so much about me?' She dragged her arm away, rubbing her wrist to erase the burning touch, wishing she could wipe away the pain she felt at the coldly arrogant assertion. 'I'm sorry to disappoint you but I don't give a damn what you do or don't remember! That's all in the past and that's where it is going to remain!'

'Is that right? Somehow it doesn't seem so simple to separate the past and the present any longer.' He stared down at her in silence. 'It would be easy to pick up the threads again, wouldn't it, Claire? There's still a lot of feeling left between us.'

'Don't be ridiculous! My heaven, but I never fully realised before just how huge your ego is! You can't bear to think that I've got over you.'

He shrugged. 'I'm a realist. But if you want to carry on fooling yourself then be my guest. However, this does need talking through, though not here. Perhaps over dinner tonight if you're free?'

'I won't ever be free for you! Do you really imagine that I would be fool enough to fall for that?' She laughed hoarsely, her face paper-white. 'There is no way that you are manoeuvring me into another affair! If you need female companionship then find someone else, because I am not interested! The only thing we have in common is business.'

'Is it?' He moved suddenly, trapping her against the shelves, shielding her from any curious eyes as he stood in front of her so close that she could feel the heat from his body. For a silent moment he stared into her eyes then smiled slowly as his gaze dropped deliberately to her mouth in a look she could feel. 'You say that with such fervour, Claire, yet I find it difficult to believe it.' He ran a finger softly down her cheek, triumph gleaming in his eyes when he heard her swift intake of breath.

Claire closed her eyes then pushed him away, her heart aching at the deliberate way he was trying to torment her. 'Then I suggest you try harder. I'm not interested in anything you have to say unless it's related to business.'

'I see. In that case I'd better tell you what I came to

before I got side-tracked.' He leant easily against the wooden panelling, composed, assured, unperturbed by what had happened and her obvious anger, and that more than anything enabled Claire to get a grip on her emotions.

'And that was?' she asked.

'That I've been making arrangements for you to fly to the New York store next week.'

'New York? But. . .I don't understand. Why do you want me to go there?' It was hard to follow this sudden switch in conversation from personal to business.

'Experience. You will be taking over the department soon so now seems like the ideal opportunity for you to get some idea of how our other branches operate. One of the major failings here has been the lack of any ongoing training programme. I mean to rectify that. New York has been directed to undertake a valentine project too so that it would be invaluable experience for you to compare their ideas with your own at first hand.'

'I see. But when would you want me to go?' She glanced round uncertainly. 'I want to get this under way first.'

'Naturally, but it should be up and running by next week. I can't claim that all the American sales techniques would work here but we can all learn a lot from them. So what do you say?'

'Well, yes. Obviously I would love to go.' Her mind was working overtime. What a marvellous opportunity it would be not only to learn about the other store but to get away from Cal for a time and give herself a breathing-space. That was all she needed, of course—a few days to get herself back in hand. He was no longer a part of her life and she accepted that; it was just the fact that he was always around that had been proving so difficult to handle lately.

'Good.' He turned to go then stopped, glancing back at her, something about his expression that made her new-found optimism waver. 'I forgot to mention that I shall be flying out there with you.'

'You will?' It was impossible to hide her shock. It felt as though the ground had just fallen away beneath her, leaving her teetering on the edge of some vast chasm.

'Mmm, there's a few problems that need my attention so I thought we may as well make the journey together. It isn't a problem, is it?'

The mockery in his eyes told her that he knew that it was, but she'd be damned if she'd admit it! 'No.'

'Well, that's settled, then. I'll let you have all the details.'

Claire murmured a response then turned away, making a great performance out of clearing up the mess from the display. He had sounded so businesslike as he'd explained his reasons for this trip but that glint in his eyes warned her that he might have other, different ideas. Well, if he had then he was going to be sorely disappointed! Oh, she wasn't fool enough to imagine that he had been harbouring thoughts of turning back the clock because he *cared* about her. Far from it. From what she could see, Michael Callan's ego was the only thing suffering here. He didn't like to think that she was no longer interested in him, and that made him dangerous, but she'd be prepared. This was a business trip and by heaven it was going to stay a business trip. She'd make certain of that!

CHAPTER THREE

'CHAMPAGNE, madam. . .sir?'

'Just coffee, black, please. Claire?'

'I'll have the champagne, thank you.' Claire accepted the glass, wrinkling her nose as she took a sip of the wine. She didn't really like champagne but maybe it would do the trick of quieting her nerves. She set the glass down on the lap-top table and glanced at Cal, who was engrossed in his paperwork. This was probably all old hat to him but for her it was a whole new experience. She'd never dreamt that they would fly Concorde to New York!

He looked up, smiling at the shimmer of excitement in her eyes. 'Not sorry that you agreed to come?'

'Of course not!' She bit her lip, realising she had responded instinctively to the warmth in his deep voice. 'I'm looking forward to learning all I can from the trip.'

'Of course.' Mockery gleamed in the depths of his green eyes as he put down his pen and lifted the cup to his lips. 'That is the only reason why you've come, isn't it?'

'Yes!' She picked up her glass, annoyed that he could stir these feelings inside her so easily. Was she being overly sensitive or had that note of warmth been deliberate?

She glanced back at him, her temper rising when she saw the expression on his face. 'Stop that! I don't know what's going on inside your head and frankly I don't want to, but I only agreed to come for the sake of business!'

'Did I say anything to imply otherwise? I'm hurt, Claire, that you seem to have this low opinion of my motives. Why do you feel like that?'

'Why?' She laughed shortly. 'I imagine it owes something to what happened three years ago!'

'It might surprise you to learn that I did what I did with the best of intentions.' The mockery faded abruptly, his eyes level as they met hers. Claire could see herself reflected in their clear green depths, as though he was drawing her inside him, sapping her will as he had done once before, but she was older now and wiser. She wouldn't allow him to trick her with soft words.

'You expect me to believe that?' She shook her head. 'Sorry, Cal, but I gave up believing in fairy-stories some time back, around the time that you decided to end our relationship. . .for the very best of intentions, of course.'

He sighed softly as he set the cup back down. 'I never intended for you to get hurt, Claire.'

'How did you imagine that I would feel? Grateful that you'd suddenly decided to tell me the truth? We were living together, Cal. I thought that implied a degree of commitment, not to mention honesty on both sides. Yet I go home to find you with your bags packed, calmly announcing that you were a member of the Hadley family and that our relationship was finished!' She was shaking with anger and pain. This was the last thing she had wanted to happen but there was no way she could let it pass. 'I would feel more respect for you if you just told the truth instead of making up these stories about doing it for my benefit.'

'And the plain truth is that I never wanted to hurt you.' There was anger in his voice now. 'You don't understand the circumstances, so don't be so hasty to pass judgement.'

'Hasty? I've hardly been that. I've had three years to form my opinion of you, three years to work out how any decent human being could treat another the way you treated me! Oh, it was slickly done, obviously well planned and just as well executed. You had your bags packed and were gone almost before I knew what was happening, avoiding any unpleasant scenes. You must have had a lot of practice at doing it, Cal. Or is it just that you are a born bast——?'

'Don't!' He gripped her arm, his fingers bruising. 'You aren't doing yourself any favours by talking like this.'

'Is that a threat?' She laughed hoarsely, twisting her arm free of his grasp. 'What do you intend to do, Mr Callan—dismiss me for impertinence? Well, for your information I could quite easily get another job! I did toy with the idea three years ago, even went as far as accepting an interview at another store, but then I thought, Why should I? Why should I leave and have to start afresh, make new friends, work from the bottom again? *I* hadn't done anything wrong!' She smoothed her hair back, her eyes skimming his face with contempt. 'But perhaps you were merely threatening to withhold this promotion from me. Surely that would mean a lot of awkward explanations for you?'

'I think not.' He sat back, his face cold. 'You seem to forget that I control this company. No one would question a decision I made about the future of an employee, although they might wonder what you had done to deserve it. You might find it a lot harder to get another job than you imagine. However, I wasn't making any threats. I can't make you believe me, Claire, I can only repeat that you don't understand the circumstances behind what happened.' He picked up his pen, his glance impersonal now. 'There is a board meeting today so we shall be going directly to the store once we land.'

He turned back to his work and Claire sank back in her seat, closing her eyes against the sudden sting of tears. She'd been so determined to handle this trip coolly and professionally, yet look what had happened now.

'Don't brood, Claire. It doesn't help anything.'

She blinked back the tears. 'It's difficult not to brood, Cal. The past seems to be at the root of all our disagreements recently. Not very professional, is it?' She made a shaky attempt at a laugh, freezing as he leant over and gently wiped a tear from her cheek.

'You're only human, Claire. You can't help your feelings.'

'Not even when they get in the way of business? That doesn't sound like the Michael Callan who's built himself the reputation of being a ruthless businessman who *never* allows emotion to influence his decisions.' She moved away, wiping her eyes with her hands.

'Perhaps I haven't had the time to be anything else. When I took over control of Hadley's it was about to go under. It took all my time and all my concentration to save it. Emotion hasn't been a luxury I've been able to afford, but that doesn't mean that I am unfeeling.' His eyes drifted softly over her face, darkening to a smoky green as they met hers. 'I remember what we had, Claire. Breaking up was the hardest decision I've ever had to make.'

His low, deep voice was lighting fires inside her again, flames that threatened what little composure she had left. She drew in a shuddering breath, her eyes filled with pain. 'But you still made that decision, Cal. You say that I don't understand; I say that's just an excuse. I no longer fitted in with your plans so end of story, and end of our relationship. Oh, I'll admit that I was devastated, but I've got over it now. So don't worry about me, not when you have more important things to think about.'

'Does anyone really get over a lost love-affair? Isn't it more accurate to say that it lingers at the back of one's mind, a tantalising memory full of regrets?' He smiled almost sadly. 'The problem is that in this case no amount of regrets could have changed the outcome. I was forced to make a decision, but that doesn't mean that I don't remember what we had and often wish things could have turned out differently.'

'But they didn't so there seems little point in dwelling on it.' She beckoned to the flight attendant to refill her glass, effectively putting an end to the disturbing conversation, but it wasn't easy to put it out of her mind. Had Cal been telling the truth about being forced to end their relationship? If he had then it opened up a floodgate of possibilities that kept her busy until they came in to land.

She sighed as she watched him pack up his papers. What did it matter now? What they'd once had was all in the past.

* * *

'And best and last is my department. Not that I'm biased, of course, Claire!'

Claire laughed. She'd taken an immediate liking to Brandon White, her opposite number at the New York store. He had taken her on a full tour of the huge building and now her head was reeling with impressions of vastness and luxury. She turned slowly on her heel, admiring the huge crystal chandeliers that hung from the ceiling, waterfalls of sculptured glass that reflected rainbows of light on to the smoked-glass mirrored columns.

'I've never seen anything like this! It's so vast, so luxurious. It makes the London store look like something from the Dark Ages!'

Brandon smiled, running a hand over his perfectly cut brown hair. 'It might surprise you to learn that a lot of our customers would love to shop at the London store. I've seen photographs of it and I must say that I find all that elegant old wood and sense of history far more attractive than all this gloss.' He shook his head. 'Don't get me wrong. This is a great store and Cal has done a fantastic job over the past few years, but London! It has to be my dream to work there.'

Claire laughed again, ruefully. 'I suppose it's just a case of familiarity breeding contempt. You're right, there is a timeless elegance about the London branch, but that doesn't mean that I don't enjoy a bit of "gloss" now and then. And as for your valentine promotion—well, it's lovely.'

'The original idea was yours, I believe.' Brandon led the way to where a small garden had been laid, complete with trees and miniature waterfall and flower-decked gazebo. 'We were planning on doing something but went to town after we'd received Cal's directive. I'm particularly pleased with this display of valentine cards on loan from one of our museums. Take a look at this one designed by the British artist Kate Greenaway. It was printed around the 1880s. Then there's this from the Civil War period, around 1861. I doubt anyone would find a tent romantic nowadays but when you lift those tent flaps you can see a Union soldier kneeling by a table writing to his sweetheart back home. Here, let me unlock the case so that you can see it properly.'

He opened the glass case, watching as Claire gently raised the tent flaps on the card. 'It's lovely. So touching that even in wartime men and women still sent their cards. And look at this one. The satin is still so fresh, and is that real lace the frame is made from?'

'It is. That's one of my favourites also. It dates from around 1850 and was produced by Esther A. Howland, one of the first US valentine manufacturers. It uses a theme that was popular then, a couple in an idealised country setting, plus the obligatory heart, of course.'

'It's a pity that no one makes cards like this today.' Claire stood aside while Brandon re-locked the case.

'They do. We have a display of them right over here.' He led her to the counter, lifting a card out of the glass display front. 'There are several artists making cards for us during the promotion but this must be one of the best.'

Claire took it carefully, inspecting the delicate arrangement of pressed flowers and lace, the exquisite penmanship inside. 'It's beautiful. Is it expensive?'

'Depends what you call expensive.' He named a

sum, laughing at her expression as she converted the dollars into sterling.

'That's expensive! Surely you don't sell that many of them?'

'You'd be surprised. The type of customer who shops here not only has the money but the need to spend it. We sold over a hundred similar cards yesterday and expect to sell several thousand during the promotion, all at a tidy profit.'

'And that is why I thought you should come here, Claire. The London store has been in danger of letting its standards drop but that isn't what a Hadley's customer wants. There are plenty of run-of-the-mill shops around but few high-class ones.'

She stiffened as she heard Cal's voice. They'd come straight to the store, where he had handed her over to Brandon before he had left for his meeting. Now just the sound of his voice sent all those unsettling quivers of awareness racing up and down her spine again, putting her instantly on the defensive.

'I understand that, but I doubt if our customers in London would pay so much for a card.' There was a note of challenge in her voice and she felt Brandon look at her in surprise.

'And that is the heart of the problem. Not the customer's unwillingness to pay, but the staff's blinkered attitude. Hopefully this trip will help you overcome that, Claire.'

There was no mistaking the rebuke and she flushed, staring coldly back at him. 'I am willing to learn if it will improve my effectiveness in the job. However, I think you too have things to learn, Cal. American marketing techniques won't always work in England.'

'We shall see.'

He moved away, his face set as he walked over to the garden area. Claire let out a shuddering sigh, smiling with embarrassment when Brandon said softly, 'I never thought I'd live to see the day when that guy lost his cool. What is it with you two, Claire? You could have cut the atmosphere with a knife just now!'

'We. . .we just rub each other up the wrong way occasionally.'

'And that's all it is?' He held his hand up to stave off her protests. 'OK, I believe you. I'm just glad that's the way things are. It means I can safely ask you out tonight without stepping on any toes. So how about it, Claire? Dinner, maybe a club, just to welcome you to the Big Apple, you understand?'

His brown eyes were filled with warmth and Claire smiled. 'I'd like that very much, thank—'

'But unfortunately you will have to pass up the invitation. I've already made plans for the evening, Claire.'

Twin spots of colour burned in her cheeks at the arrogant statement. 'I hadn't realised that dining with you was part of the schedule?'

Cal smiled tauntingly, obviously amused by her anger. 'It isn't. However, I've made arrangements for you to meet with a couple of buyers from our Miami branch who are in town at the moment. Naturally I expect you to fall in with the arrangements. I'm sure Brandon can alter his plans accordingly.'

It was an order, not a request and they all knew it. For a second Claire was tempted to argue, but what was the point? She was here on business and if he chose to fill her every waking moment with work then she had to go along with him. 'Whatever you say. However, I shall need to get changed. Can you call me a cab to take me to my hotel, please?'

She directed the request at Brandon, but it was Cal who answered. 'You don't need a cab. You'll be staying here in the penthouse suite. Show her where it is when you're through here, Brandon.'

He walked away, mingling with the crowd of elegant shoppers. Claire counted to ten, unwilling to make a fool of herself, but there was no way she could leave unasked the question that was nagging inside her head. 'Who usually uses the penthouse suite?'

There was a faint but marked hesitation before Brandon replied, speculation in the look he gave her now. 'Cal. He lives there. It appears that you two will be sharing.'

Claire clenched her hands. Abruptly she turned away to avoid the man's gaze, staring after Cal with desperation in her eyes. What was he up to now? What?

CHAPTER FOUR

THE knock came at the door just as she was putting the finishing touches to her make-up. Claire stepped back from the mirror then paused to study her reflection.

The black velvet suit had been wickedly expensive, an impulsive purchase made only that morning before they had left for the airport. Now she was glad that she had bought it. It emphasised her slender figure and served as the perfect foil for her blonde hair, lending her a cool sophistication she was grateful for. She would need every bit of help she could get to last through the coming evening in Cal's company.

'Are you ready yet, Claire?'

As ready as she was ever going to be! With one last, confidence-boosting glance in the mirror she went over to the door and opened it. 'Yes. Do we have to leave now?'

'In a few minutes or so. They'll ring through when the car arrives. Would you like a drink before we go?'

She shook her head, moving past him into the huge central sitting area that separated the two bedrooms with their en-suite bathrooms. Cal hadn't been in when she'd arrived at the penthouse and she'd taken time to explore the apartment, trying to convince herself that it would be less intimate sharing this vast space than sharing adjoining hotel bedrooms, but it hadn't worked. At least in a hotel there would be other people about while here they were completely alone.

'No, thank you, not after that champagne I had earlier.'

He followed her into the room, the thick palest grey carpet absorbing his footsteps as he walked over to the bar. 'Please yourself, but I doubt if a couple of glasses of wine will have had a lingering effect.'

'Probably not, but I prefer to keep a clear head for a business meeting.' She sat down on one of the huge dusky blue sofas, crossing her sheer-clad legs as she watched him pour whisky into a cut-glass tumbler. Everything in the apartment was the best that money could buy and at any other time Claire would have enjoyed staying in such luxurious surroundings, but now she was too tense to relax.

'Ah, yes, business. Of course.' He took a swallow of the whisky then swirled it around the glass. He was wearing a dark lounge suit and white shirt with a discreetly patterned silk tie, clothes that bore all the hallmarks of civilisation, but when he looked up suddenly there was nothing civilised about the expression in his glittering green eyes.

Claire's heart leapt in an instinctive response. She stood up abruptly and walked to the window, willing herself to stay calm, but it was impossible to stem the shudder that ran through her when she heard him put down the glass.

He came to stand behind her, his reflection merging with hers in the mirror-dark glass. It was like a flashback to the past to see them standing there like that, and she felt her heart ache with a fresh grief. She had loved him so much, but in the end it hadn't been enough to hold him.

'It isn't easy, is it, Claire?'

His voice was deep, warmly intimate, making her tingle with a heady longing. She closed her eyes, trying desperately not to respond to the seductive quality, but that was like asking a flower not to open to the sun or a bee not to search for nectar. There was no way that she could ignore him and pretend that she didn't understand what he meant.

'No, it isn't easy.' She shrugged lightly, her shoulder-blades brushing the hard wall of his chest. 'But then who said that life should be easy?'

'And who said that it should be this difficult? There is an answer to this, Claire.' He turned her slowly to stare intently into her face.

'Is there? From where I'm standing I can't seem to see one.' She laughed shakily, more disturbed by the glitter in his darkening green eyes than she cared to admit.

'That's because you aren't thinking logically.' He smiled almost tenderly at her, his hand moving to her cheek to stroke the smooth fine skin. 'It's really quite straightforward.'

The touch of his hand was making her dizzy. It seemed to be drawing the strength from her limbs and the ability to think from her mind. Every bit of her seemed to be centred on that one small area where his hand smoothed so slowly, so insistently across her flesh. 'I. . .I don't understand, Cal.'

'Then let me explain. We take up where we left off.' His hand stilled against the underside of her jaw where a pulse was beating rapidly in mute betrayal of her vulnerability. It seemed to please him because he smiled with a touch of arrogance. 'There is still something there between us, Claire—that's obvious, so why keep on pretending there isn't? It was good between us once and I see no reason why it shouldn't be so again.'

'And what if it doesn't work out? What then?' Coldness was stealing through her, a coldness born out of horror. She couldn't believe what she was hearing, couldn't believe that he would suggest such a thing!

He must have caught an echo of it in her voice because he bent closer. 'Then we call it a day. We aren't two young kids any more. We're two adults who can decide what we want from life and if we make mistakes then we can rectify them. Surely it isn't a crime to see if we can enjoy the same sort of happiness we once shared?'

'No, it isn't a crime. It's the crassest suggestion I've ever heard! Do you really imagine that I would willingly start another affair with you after last time?' She swatted his hand away, her blue eyes filled with fire. 'Thank you but no, thank you. I'm not interested!'

His face tightened, his eyes narrowing to glittering pin-points of ice. 'That isn't the impression you've been handing out!' He dragged her into his arms, his hand moving over the soft folds of velvet to close over her breasts, triumph on his face when he felt her rigid nipple pushing into his palm. 'You can lie all you like, sweet Claire, but your body can't. See how it responds to me, see how it still longs for my touch?'

He caressed her through the soft fabric, teasing the nipple into a throbbing peak of desire that sent waves of bitter-sweet longing flooding through her. This was the very thing she had been dreading might happen, betraying how easily he could make her respond to his touch, but she would never admit it to him!

'You flatter yourself, Cal. As you just said, neither

of us is inexperienced now. Naturally I respond to your touch as I would to any attractive man. Passion once awoken is hard to subdue, so why try?' She forced a hint of cool amusement to her expression as she stared back at him. 'You were my first lover, Cal, but don't make the mistake of thinking you are the only one. That could lead to a great deal of disappointment. Now if you have quite finished practising your seduction techniques, would you mind letting me go? I don't want to waste time re-doing my make-up.'

Had she gone too far? She held her breath as she watched the expressions that crossed his face, ranging from disbelief to anger, to finally a wry acceptance. With a mocking bow he let her go, watching silently as she sat down on the sofa again.

Claire steeled herself to meet his gaze, feeling the pain gnawing inside her. She had sworn never to let him hurt her again but what he'd just suggested had almost torn her heart in two. When he made no attempt to speak, she raised a delicate golden brow, keeping the hurt out of her voice. 'Don't tell me that I have actually managed to take the wind out of your sails?'

He laughed deeply, walking over to the bar to pick up his glass. 'Not quite, although I do confess to feeling a trifle surprised.'

'At what? That I should refuse your tempting offer?' She smoothed her hand over the velvet skirt, making furrows in the pile with her fingertips.

'No. Contrary to your opinion of me I'm not that vain. What surprises me, Claire, is that you should show such little outward sign of all those lovers.' He let his gaze skim over her, openly assessing her slender curves in a look that brought the colour to her face.

'You still look as untouched and innocent as I remember you, but it just goes to show how deceptive appearances can be, because now it seems you are a woman of the world.'

He didn't believe her? Her heart turned over at the thought and she stood up abruptly. 'Frankly, Cal, that is the most sexist statement I've ever heard! Why should I *look* any different?' Her eyes skimmed his face but she found it impossible to hold that glittering green gaze for longer than a heartbeat. 'If you want the truth then neither do you look any different, but I doubt if you've led a monk-like existence these past three years!'

She hadn't meant it to come out that way, not with jealousy echoing in her voice. He smiled slowly, putting down the glass with a deliberation that set her nerves on edge before he moved towards her. 'No, I can't claim to have been a monk, but neither can I claim to have been living the life of a rake either. You, Claire, were a hard act to follow and I found that when I did have time to spare from keeping the business afloat I didn't have much inclination. It's difficult to make love to a woman when your head is full of pictures of another.'

He bent and brushed her lips with his in a kiss so brief that it was over before Claire had a chance to object. She touched a finger to her mouth, staring up at him with confusion in her eyes, and saw him smile in a way that made everything inside her flare to life. Emotion flowed between them, touching him, touching her, joining them with an invisible bond, and she half raised her hand to reach out to him when the telephone rang.

She drew in a tiny, shuddering breath, watching as

Cal went to answer it. Saved by the bell, but saved from what? From making a complete and utter fool of herself by giving him what he wanted? Had he been telling the truth just now or had it been a way of manipulating her again? She wished she knew, because it was becoming increasingly difficult to fight not just him but herself as well.

The restaurant was elegant and expensive, situated in New York's Little Italy district and filled with the cream of society. Claire studied the other well-dressed diners then let her eyes drift back to the man at her side, her heart leaping when she found that he was watching her. It had kept happening all night long—she would look up to find Cal's eyes on her—and now her nerves were raw.

The coffee-cup rattled against the saucer as she set it down and she felt rather than saw the smile Cal gave. He knew how she was feeling, knew that she was dreading the time when they would have to return to the apartment for the night. Had he been planning this all along, right from the moment he had suggested this trip? Frankly, she wouldn't put it past him!

'I'm going to the rest-room, Claire. Would you like to come?'

The softly voiced question broke into her disturbing thoughts. Claire turned to smile in relief at Cathy Davies, one of the buyers from Miami. 'Oh, yes, please. Lead the way.'

The rest-room was empty when they walked in. Claire set her bag down then took out her lipstick, cursing as she smudged lipstick on her upper lip because her hands were shaking.

'Here.' Cathy handed her a tissue from the box set on the marble counter, smiling faintly. 'Not that it's any wonder your hands are shaking. You could cut the atmosphere between you and Cal with a knife. Forgive me for being nosy, but are you *really* here to learn about American marketing techniques?'

Claire's hand slipped again, setting another peach-tinted smear on her upper lip. Deliberately, she wiped it away, using the few seconds it took to find some dismissive answer to the question, but it was impossible to think up a convincing lie. 'I thought I was.'

'But now you're starting to wonder if the game-plan has altered?' Cathy laughed as she opened her bag and took out a compact. 'I never thought I would live to see the day when the Ice Man started to melt.'

'What do you mean? Are you referring to Cal?' There was no way that Claire could hide her surprise and Cathy laughed again.

'Of course! And the fact that you have never thought of him that way only serves to emphasise the very point I'm making.' She snapped the compact shut then looked at Claire. 'I am just one of many women who have done their utmost to attract Cal's attention, one of the many *disappointed* women, to be precise. He's been polite, friendly, charming in that coolly British way, but never once has he shown a single ounce of real emotion. . .until tonight! I tell you, honey, the air fairly sizzles when he looks at you. Tell me what your secret is and I'll have it patented.'

Claire laughed, unable to take offence at such friendly teasing. 'There's no secret. Cal—well, Cal and I did have something going for us once but it's past history. All we have in common now is business.'

'If that's business then where have I gone wrong? That man looks at you in a way that makes my toes curl. Take it from one who would dearly love to step in your shoes that the last thing he has on his mind is business!'

Claire's face went pale. 'I don't care what he has on his mind. No power on earth would make me get involved with him again on a personal level!'

'You still love him that much, huh? Never mind, honey, I'm sure it will work out in the end.' She patted Claire's hand kindly then headed out of the door, missing the shock etched on Claire's pale face. The door swung to but Claire stayed where she was, listening to the drumming beat of her heart, the echo of Cathy's words beating inside her head.

She loved Cal. That was why she had been so afraid since he'd come back into her life, and it had taken the perception of a stranger to make her face the fact. Now all she could do was make sure that he never found out how she felt.

The wind was bitter, gusting along the street, knifing through the soft folds of the velvet suit. Claire shivered as she hurried towards the door while Cal finished speaking to the driver. The limousine drove away and he turned to follow her, digging the key out of his pocket to unlock the side-door. The wind blew his hair back from his forehead, leaving his face stark in the cold glow of the security lights, and just for a weak moment Claire allowed her eyes to feast on the sight of him before hurriedly dropping her gaze as he turned to her.

'Let's get inside. You look half frozen. I should have

warned you to wear a coat. New York in February is one of the coldest places I know.'

He put a hand to the small of her back to guide her ahead of him into the small private hallway that gave access to the lift that went solely to the penthouse suite. Claire moved away as soon as they were inside, ignoring the mocking tilt to his mouth. She didn't care what he thought; there was still tonight to get through, and all the other nights until she returned to London. She had to make it clear that, no matter what he had planned, she had no intention of sleeping with him!

'Don't look so worried, Claire. I don't intend to pounce on you once we're upstairs.' He leant against the wall, his hands pushed into his trouser pockets, his tie hanging loosely, his black hair mussed from the wind, looking so devastatingly attractive that Claire could have wept. It took all her strength to stare coldly back at him.

'I never imagined that you would. *Pouncing* isn't your style, Cal!'

He laughed at the stinging retort. 'You know me too well, Claire. It takes all the surprise out of what I do.'

'Oh, I expect you can still surprise me if you really think it worth trying, but let's lay our cards on the table. I will not sleep with you. So save your breath and my time because nothing you can do or say will make me change my mind.'

'Nothing?' He straightened slowly, his eyes holding hers for a moment that hummed with tension. 'Is it wise to issue a challenge like that? I could find it tempting to take you up on it.'

'It wasn't meant to be a challenge! I just wanted you to understand how I feel.' Anger rippled through her, anger that was intensified by a strange, disturbing excitement which she tried her hardest to suppress. 'I resent the fact that you've placed me in this position. You know I only agreed to this trip because I believed it to be purely for business! I didn't come to provide you with a few hours' amusement. Even Cathy noticed the—' She broke off, her face colouring as she realised how it would sound.

'Cathy noticed. . .what?' He spoke quietly but there was a steely note of authority in his voice. 'Has she been saying something to upset you, Claire?'

'No. Forget it.'

'But I don't want to forget it. Obviously she's said something about me and I want to know what it is.'

'Why?' She glared back at him. 'Afraid that she might have said something to damage your reputation? Don't worry, Cal. Cathy is a fan of yours even though she does find that cool composure of yours hard to swallow. What was it that she called you?' She pretended to think for a moment, enjoying the mounting annoyance on his face. 'Ah, yes, that's it: the Ice Man. Mmm, she could be right. There is something decidedly cold and calculating about you, Michael Callan, as I know better than most.'

'Do you? But when was I ever cold with you, Claire?' He moved suddenly, trapping her against the wall as he stood in front of her. 'Our relationship was red-hot from the word go, from what I remember of it. Don't tell me that time has dimmed your memory? Maybe it could do with a refresher, my sweet.'

He bent towards her, intent written all over his face, but Claire turned her head away to avoid the kiss. 'I don't need any refreshers, thank you. I recall exactly how it was between us, and how it ended: coldly, calculatedly, the Ice Man at his best!'

The lift hummed to a stop and she slid away from him to step inside, feeling her heart pounding. She shouldn't let him goad her like that but she'd always found it impossible to ignore him. He had this knack of arousing her to anger just as easily as he'd always aroused her to passion.

'Seems to me that you and I need to talk. It's about time I explained why I had to end our relationship so abruptly.'

'I'm not interested! The time for explanations is long past, Cal. Nothing is going to change the past, especially not talking about it, not when we can barely manage to say half a dozen civil words to one another before we end up arguing.'

'We always did argue, Claire.' He turned the key to set the lift in motion, leaning casually against the panelled wall as he watched her. 'But making up afterwards made all those arguments worthwhile. Perhaps that's what this is leading up to right now—a quarrel that we can patch up in that highly satisfactory way?'

He was so smugly self-assured that she could have hit him! 'No way! You might have tricked me into staying in the apartment with you but that's as far as it goes. There won't be any attempts at making up!'

'I didn't trick you into staying here. I just didn't relish the thought of you being alone in some hotel. New York is a dangerous place for a woman alone. I wouldn't have been able to rest wondering what might be happening to you.'

There was no doubting his sincerity. Claire felt

warmed by his concern even though that was the last way she wanted to feel. No matter what she really felt for Cal she couldn't blind herself to the truth that he would use any vulnerability she displayed to get what he wanted. And in this case it seemed that he wanted her!

'How sweet! I suppose I should feel flattered, Cal, that you show such concern for an employee, but then I expect it's really because you don't want all the inconvenience if anything did happen to me. Isn't that right?' There was a nice ring of scorn in her voice which she felt proud of until she saw the anger that flashed across his face.

'One of these days, lady, that sharp little tongue of yours is going to get you into trouble.' He smiled wolfishly, moving slowly and deliberately towards her so that she backed hurriedly against the wall.

'Look, Cal, don't you think this is——?'

'Trying to talk your way out of it now, are you, my love?' He shook his head, his hand sliding around the back of her neck as he pulled her towards him. 'Don't bother. It's far too late for that now!'

His lips were hot and demanding as they met hers in a kiss that seemed to shake her to the very depths of her soul. For a moment, Claire resisted, but it was merely a token resistance when everything inside her was urging her to kiss him back. With a tiny, helpless moan she opened her mouth, feeling his body surge against hers as he deepened the kiss until she was breathless and clinging to him. This was what it had all been leading to, all the arguments, all the tension—to this moment when Cal held her and kissed her as though nothing else in the world mattered.

When the ground suddenly shuddered beneath their feet it seemed right, as though nature was as affected by the moment as they were. It was only when Cal lifted his head and swore softly that Claire realised something was wrong. She stared round in confusion, suddenly aware that they were no longer moving.

'Why have we stopped? We can't have reached the penthouse yet, surely?' She glanced at the indicator panel, but there were no lights gleaming to show which level they were at.

Cal punched a button on the controls, his face grim when nothing happened. 'No. We appear to be stuck halfway.'

'Halfway. . .you mean that the lift has broken down? But Cal. . . Oh!' She gasped as the lights went out, plunging them into darkness.

'It's all right. The emergency lighting will come on in a second. There.' He smiled reassuringly at her as dim lights glowed in the ceiling and Claire fought down the momentary panic.

'So what do we do now?' she asked quietly.

'Not a lot. We shall have to wait for someone to sort the trouble out.' He loosened his tie and unbuttoned the neck of his shirt then sat down on the floor. 'You may as well make yourself comfortable, Claire. This could turn out to be a long night.'

Claire stared at him for a long, silent moment then looked round the confines of the small lift and swallowed. There was no 'could' about it. This was going to be a very long night indeed!

CHAPTER FIVE

IT WAS so hot.

Claire ran a hand over her face, wiping the perspiration from her upper lip before resting her head back and closing her eyes.

'Are you all right? You look very pale.'

Cal spoke softly, his voice barely disturbing the silence, but she still jumped nervously. She looked over at where he was sitting, his back propped against the lift wall. He had stripped off his jacket and shirt and now she could see beads of perspiration caught in the thick tangle of black hair that covered his muscular chest, evidence that he was feeling just as hot and uncomfortable as she was; but that was the only outward sign. Resting easily against the wall, his long legs taking up most of the small floor space, he looked totally relaxed. Did nothing dent his iron-clad composure?

Panic rose inside her all at once and she forced herself to concentrate on answering the question to keep it at bay. 'I'm fine. Just rather hot, that's all.'

His eyes narrowed assessingly on the black velvet suit before returning to her pale, strained face. 'You'd feel a whole lot more comfortable if you took that jacket off, Claire. It's stifling in here and it will probably get worse before too long. The heating system isn't linked to the power so it won't switch off.'

She shook her head, brushing away a damp strand of

hair that clung to her cheek. 'I'll be fine. It can't be much longer before they fix it, surely? How long have we been stuck here now?'

Cal glanced at the wafer-thin gold watch strapped to his wrist. 'A little over an hour, but you have to face facts, Claire. There's no saying if anyone even knows that we're here seeing as the alarm doesn't seem to be working.'

'But somebody *must* know that the lift is stuck between floors!'

There was desperation in her voice and Cal stood up, his face set as he pressed the red alarm button again. 'We can only hope that they do, but this lift is solely for the use of anyone staying in the penthouse. The security staff don't need to come into this part of the building when they know I'm here.'

'That's ridiculous!' The strain was making her edgy, ready to snap at the least provocation. 'I would have thought it was common sense to keep a check on what was going on here.'

'When I'm away obviously that is what happens but when I'm using the apartment I prefer not to have people intruding on my privacy.'

Especially not when it might prove a shade awkward! 'I see. What a pity that you can't find some place else to entertain your ladyfriends! Then maybe we wouldn't be in this situation. Routine security checks would be merely a sensible precaution, not an invasion of your precious privacy!'

He laughed deeply, moving over to sit on the floor beside her. 'I thought *I* was the one with green eyes!' He tapped her cheek gently with a long finger, smiling into her angry face. 'Not that I'm objecting. I find your jealousy rather flattering if you'd like the truth.'

'I am not jealous! You can get that out of your head right away. I was merely making an observation, a wholly justifiable one in the circumstances.'

'Mmm, so you say. I'd debate that with you if I didn't know it would be a sheer waste of effort. I get the impression lately that you'd call black white if it would promote an argument with me. You really should try to keep a rein on your temper, Claire.'

He was mocking her quite deliberately and, while Claire knew it, it seemed impossible to stem the angry flood of words. 'I have never had any trouble with my temper before! It's just you, Michael Callan. You seem to be deliberately trying to annoy me!'

'Do I?' His expression altered subtly, his eyes darkening as they traced her face. 'And have you asked yourself why that could be?'

'I. . . No!' The way he was looking at her made her feel suddenly afraid. She scrambled to her feet and crossed the lift to press the alarm bell, slamming her hand against the panel when it remained silent. 'Oh, why won't it work? Can't you do something?'

'Such as?' He looked up at the ceiling, squinting against the yellow glow from the emergency lighting. 'We're stuck somewhere between the fifteenth and sixteenth floors, I'd guess. I suppose it might be possible for me to get out into the shaft and see if I can climb to the next floor.' He stood up and flexed the heavy muscles in his shoulders as he started to reach for the trapdoor set in the lift roof.

'No!' She caught his arm, her hands fastening around the warm, faintly damp flesh, feeling sick with fear at the thought of him taking such a risk. 'You could get hurt, Cal. I won't let you do it!'

'I didn't think you cared one way or the other what happens to me, Claire.' There was a note in his deep voice that sent a warning *frisson* racing down her spine, but for some strange reason she chose not to heed it.

'Of course I care.' She took a slow, deep breath, fighting to keep the pictures of him lying hurt and helpless from her mind, but it was impossible to drive them away. Her hands clung to him, tightening around the firm flesh of his upper arm, feeling the warmth of his skin, the hard outline of muscle over bone.

'Do you, Claire? Do you really care?'

What was there in his voice that made her heart start to beat like crazy? She didn't know and suddenly didn't care as she looked up straight into his eyes. It was like drowning in a sea of darkening green, like being drawn deeper and deeper into fathomless depths. She looked away, willing herself to fight this attraction she felt for him, but when she looked back at him she knew it was impossible.

'Yes, I. . .I care.' Her voice was little more than a thready whisper, reluctant, hesitant, and he smiled with gentle understanding.

'The same as I care what happens to you, Claire. I always have and I always will.'

How she wanted to believe him, but there was no way she could blind herself to the truth. 'No. If you had cared then you would never have left me the way you did.'

There was a wealth of sadness in her voice and his face filled with pain. He drew her into his arms, nestling her head against the hard strength of his chest. 'I can't change what happened, Claire, just as I can't make you believe that I did it *because* I cared.'

That made no sense. She wanted desperately to ask him to explain but before she could speak he slid his hand under her chin and lifted her face, his mouth burning as he took hers in a kiss of such passion that a shudder ran through her body. For one brief moment she resisted, terrified of what would happen if she gave him the response he sought, but as his lips parted hers and his tongue slid inside her mouth to tangle with hers she knew that she was lost. If it had just been Cal she'd been fighting then maybe she could have resisted the seductive spell he was casting over her, but how could she fight against something she wanted so much herself?

'Claire, oh, Claire!' His voice was hot and rough with desire yet his hands were gentle as they dropped to the silk-covered buttons on her jacket and started to work them loose. Claire lifted her arms, running her fingers through the cool, silky dark hair at the back of his head, feathering kisses up the slanting curve of his jaw to tease the lobe of his ear. He swore softly, his impatience growing as the buttons defeated his attempts to unfasten them and she laughed gently, rubbing her lips around the curve of his ear as she stood on tiptoe, feeling the deep shudder that ran through him with a flare of heady excitement.

'Think it's funny, do you, you little witch? Teasing me like that?' There was just the faintest hint of a threat in his deep voice and she shivered delicately, wondering what form the reprisals might take.

'Mmm, you never used to have so much trouble with a few buttons, Cal.' Her mouth moved again, leaving his ear to skim along his cheekbone, her lips parting as she pressed tiny fleeting kisses to his skin. He drew in a heavy breath, his hands lifting to catch her face and hold it while he kissed her hard until she was the one who shuddered with longing. He smiled in satisfaction, his gaze scorching as it lingered on the swollen fullness of her mouth, the haze of desire that darkened her eyes almost to black.

'Do it for me, Claire. Take your jacket off.'

Such simple words, but the message in them made her shake with longing. For a moment she held his gaze then slowly let her hands drop to the buttons, watching the way his face tightened and his whole body stilled. Slowly, one by one, she worked them free, feeling the blood thundering through her veins as his eyes followed every movement of her fingers. When at last her hands dropped to her sides, he reached out, his fingers warm and gentle against her skin as he traced so lightly, so delicately down from her collarbone to her waist that she had to bite her lip to stop herself from crying out.

'Take it off, Claire. . .please.'

He tried to phrase it as a request but it came out as an order, the tension evident in the deepening timbre of his voice. Claire hesitated for a second then slowly slid the jacket down her arms, colour flowing into her face as she heard his swift indrawn breath as she finally stood in front of him clad only in the pearl-grey camisole which did little to conceal the thrusting fullness of her breasts.

'So beautiful, Claire, so very beautiful. I'd almost forgotten.' His eyes were as dark as a stormy sea as they lingered on her then lifted to meet hers in a moment that seemed to hold the whole world suspended.

Claire shuddered, more affected by the look than she could say. 'Cal, I. . .' There was just the faintest hint of fear in her soft voice, a fear not of him but of what she was doing. Would she come to regret this moment of madness all too soon? Was this really heaven within her grasp or a bitter hell?

He pressed a finger gently to her lips, his face full of understanding. 'Don't, Claire. You know you want this as much as I do.'

Tears filled her eyes and she bowed her head, unable to look at him then. 'Yes, I do, but that doesn't make it right, Cal.'

'Neither does it make it wrong.' He ran his hands lightly down her arms from shoulder to wrist, his touch so light that it felt like the brush of wings, the caress of a warm breeze, and she shivered. 'I want you, Claire. I want you more than I have ever wanted any woman, but it's your choice what happens next. Yours.'

Her choice, but which one should she make? How did one choose between heaven and heartache? She stared helplessly at him, torn in two by her needs and this fear of being hurt again as she'd been hurt before. 'Help me, Cal,' she whispered brokenly. 'Help me decide what to do!'

His face contorted and he dragged her into her arms, holding her so close that she could feel the heavy pounding of his heart against her breast, feel the evidence of his aroused body, and suddenly there was no choice to make any longer. When his hand slid up to cover her breast through the thin silk, she moaned softly, glorying in the touch of his fingers, which sent sweet waves of desire piercing through her body. Each sweep of his fingers against her flesh was driving her crazy, making her ache with a need she could no longer deny.

'Cal. . .Cal!' She whispered his name like a prayer, uncaring that he must hear her need of him in the urgency of her tone. When his head came down as he plundered her mouth with a raw, almost primitive desire, she kissed him back just as fiercely, just as demandingly. A groan tore from his lips and he moved his mouth to run a fireline of kisses across her cheek to the soft curve of her jaw, lingering on the spot at the base of her neck where a pulse was beating so desperately.

His tongue snaked out, tracing the throbbing, pulsating spot, making it beat even harder until Claire felt dizzy with the fast hammer of blood that surged along her veins. She clung to him, her fingers biting into the hardness of muscles in his shoulders, then gasped when she felt herself being lifted from the ground by strong arms wrapped around her waist. Her eyes opened straight into his, all her emotions naked to him at that moment, before he bent his head and opened his mouth over her breast, drawing the rigid nipple with its fine silk covering between his teeth.

Claire cried out, her nails biting into his flesh, her head thrown back as a sudden fierce spasm of ecstasy claimed her. The rasping feel of his tongue against the silk was lighting fires inside her, fires that burned higher and higher as he turned his attentions to her other breast, moistening the silk so that it clung to her nipple and heightened the sensations.

She was shivering when he slowly let her slide down

so that her feet touched the floor once more, every nerve raw, aching, wanting. He held her to him, his hips pressed against hers as he moved her in a rhythm that sent a flashfire of desire into the pit of her stomach. She arched against him, pressing her soft curves against the hard tautness of his body, hearing his breathing quicken.

When his hand went to the zip of her skirt she helped him, just as eager as he was to rid herself of the restriction of clothing. The skirt slid to the floor, whispering softly as it slipped over the pearl-grey silk panties, the fine mesh of her sheer stockings. Cal's hands followed its downward movement, sliding tantalisingly over her hips to stroke down her thighs, lingering on the smooth flesh above the tops of her stockings before he drew back a fraction and let his eyes enjoy what his fingers had only hinted at.

'My God, Claire, what an outfit. It's enough to drive a man wild!'

She laughed shakily, smoothing her hands across the warm roughness of his chest, letting her nails lightly graze his skin. 'I'm glad you like it.'

'I do, but I think I'd like it even more if you weren't wearing anything.' He slid his fingertips under the thin strap on her shoulder, watching her the whole time as he started to push it down so that the camisole dipped to expose one hard-tipped breast to his gaze. Claire closed her eyes, quaking shudders of longing surging inside her as she felt his knuckles brush over her bare flesh, back and forth until her breasts were throbbing and she was clinging helplessly to him.

'Cal, please. . .'

'Please what? Hold you? Kiss you?' His mouth

brushed hers as his hand moved again in another slow, deliberate sweep. 'Make love to you? That's exactly what I intend to do, my sweet.'

His hands went to his belt as he started to unbuckle it, then cursed roughly when the lift gave a sudden jolt and started to move. Claire blinked, blinded by the glare from the lights, dazed by the abrupt, shocking departure from passion.

'You'd better get these back on in case there's a reception committee waiting for us.' Cal handed her her clothes, pushing her fumbling hands aside as he helped her step into the skirt and zip it up then buttoned the jacket for her. Swiftly, he pulled his shirt on and tucked it into the waistband of his trousers just as the lift came to a halt and the doors slid open.

With a hand at her waist he guided her ahead of him, his voice icy with displeasure as he spoke to the two men waiting nervously by the lift doors. 'I shall expect a full report on this tomorrow. Now get the hell out of here.'

They went without a word, barely sparing Claire a glance, but she still felt her face start to burn with embarrassment. If Cal hadn't acted so quickly, or if the lift had restarted just a few minutes later, then there was no knowing what they might have seen!

She glanced at Cal, wondering if he too realised what a narrow escape they'd had, and felt her heart turn over when she saw the cold fury on his set face. Who was he so angry with, those men or her? Was he suddenly regretting what had happened between them and maybe blaming her for it?

Shame kept her silent as he let them into the penthouse. She walked slowly to the sitting-room and crossed to the window, resting her hot cheek against the cool glass, wishing that he would say something.

'I suggest you get to bed. It's late already thanks to that fiasco with the lift. There's a staff meeting at eight in the morning that I want you to sit in on. Goodnight.'

Was that it? Did he really think that he could walk away like that after what had happened? Claire spun round, her face pale, her eyes glittering with anger. 'Just wait a minute! Is that all you have to say, Cal?'

He stopped at once, his face devoid of emotion as he glanced back at her. 'What else is there to say? I imagine that untimely interruption has spoiled the mood for you just as it has for me, Claire.'

'That wasn't what I meant!' Her face flamed at the cold sarcasm but she faced him proudly.

'Then what do you want me to say? That I'm sorry for what happened before? That I was wrong to instigate it?' He shook his head, arrogantly male and unbending as he stood there. 'I'm afraid you'll have a long, disappointing wait if you're hoping for that. I am not in the least bit sorry. I didn't force you into anything, Claire. It was your choice, your willing choice.'

She looked away, staring down at the pale grey carpet, looking anywhere but at his cold, set face. 'I know that. I'm not trying to blame you, although I imagine you had something of the sort planned when you decided that I would stay here.'

'I explained why I wanted you here. I didn't plan anything. Now, as I said, it's very late. I suggest we leave any further discussions until tomorrow. Things often look entirely different in the clear light of day.'

He was so cold and aloof that she wanted to shake

him, wanted just once to make a dent in that damnable composure of his. 'Do they indeed? So you think that I'll wake up in the morning and realise that it was all a mistake, that I didn't *really* want to make love with you?'

A muscle ticked in his jaw but that was the only sign that she might have succeeded. 'Perhaps. It has been known to happen. We were both placed in an unusual situation tonight. It isn't surprising that things got slightly out of hand.'

Was that the way he viewed it now, as a situation that had got out of hand through circumstances? Her heart ached at the cold dismissal of what they'd shared, those tender, wonderful moments of magic, but she hid it behind a veil of anger. 'Yes, they did, but it isn't going to happen again, Cal! Understand? I didn't come here to be a. . .a plaything for you!'

'Nobody said that you did.' His eyes narrowed as he stared at her flushed face. 'You're the one jumping to conclusions, Claire.'

'Am I indeed? Well, silly me. Why on earth should I do such a thing?'

'I have no idea.'

'No? Maybe it has something to do with the way *you* have been acting, Cal.' She laughed bitterly. 'So much for this being a business trip! I think that you got me here so that you could prove just how much I still want you. Isn't that right? Your ego couldn't take the thought that I might not find you attractive any longer!'

She tossed the challenge at him, her whole body humming with tension as she waited to hear what he would say, but he said nothing, merely gave her a level look as he walked over to the bar and poured himself a brandy. He sipped it in silence then slowly set the glass down and turned back to her, and Claire felt herself grow cold at the total lack of emotion on his face.

'I asked you to come on this trip, Claire, to enhance your knowledge of the business. Personal feelings never entered into it. However, it's obvious that it is going to be a total waste of time unless we come to some sort of an agreement.'

Business, always business. It had come before everything else in the past and it came before everything now, putting their relationship exactly into the context he wanted. It made her suddenly realise what a fool she'd been to imagine it could ever change. Now all that was left to her was pride, pride not to let him see how hurt she felt.

'What sort of agreement?' she asked.

'That we forget what happened tonight and get on with the job at hand.' He picked up the glass again then took another sip of the brandy, cradling the glass in one lean hand. Claire found her eyes drawn to his hand, remembering how it had felt when he had touched her, caressed her, but she had to put such thoughts from her mind. Cal was her employer, not her lover: he might have been tempted before for whatever reason, but that didn't alter the fact that the smooth running of the business took precedence over everything else.

'That sounds perfectly all right to me. In fact I'd be only too glad to forget about it!'

'Good.' He set his glass down with a sharp clatter that might have made her think he was annoyed if she hadn't known him better. However, there was nothing in his tone to betray such feelings as he continued levelly, 'I want you to carry on here as we planned with one slight alteration.'

'And that is?' She strove to match his tone, keeping her voice as neutral as she could make it.

'That I won't be here to supervise your training. There are a few problems I need to attend to at the Miami store. I shall go down there tomorrow and I doubt if I'll be back before you return to England. However, I'm sure Brandon will be able to answer any of your queries. I shall have a word with him in the morning.'

So that was it, all cut and dried, planned out nice and neatly. She would carry on with her training while Cal would go and sort out more problems with his beloved business and both of them would forget all about what had happened tonight in the lift. Only could they? Could she forget that she loved him? Could she go back home and pretend to live a life that was in reality merely an existence? Didn't she owe it to them both to tell the truth?

'Cal, I—'

He cut her off abruptly, his face hard. 'I hope you aren't going to come up with any objections, Claire. Frankly, this seems to me the best solution to all our problems.'

Had he somehow guessed what she'd been about to say? Did he imagine that she wanted some kind of commitment from him, the same commitment he had walked away from once before? She loved him, but did she have the right to tell him that when it might be something he wouldn't want to hear?

The words died on her lips and she turned away to

walk to the door, terrified of breaking down and causing them both a great deal of embarrassment.

'Claire.'

She stopped but she didn't turn. She couldn't trust herself to turn back to him and hide what she felt. 'What is it?'

'I'm sorry.' His voice was soft and deep as it carried across the room to where she stood. Her fingers curled into her palms, digging into the soft flesh as she strove to control the instinctive response her body gave to those rich, velvet tones.

'For what?' Her own voice was thready, breathless, filled with a note of longing that echoed in the silence like a prayer. There was a moment when he seemed to hesitate, a moment when her heart stopped and her whole body stilled on a sudden surge of sweetly glorious hope, then he continued and all that sweet hope crumbled around her feet.

'For disrupting your schedule, of course.'

Her breath caught on a sob and she closed her eyes, calling herself every kind of a fool. What had she expected? That he was apologising for throwing away her love and leaving her, for putting business before all else? Would a few words of apology really have made up for all that? She didn't know. All she knew was that if any dreams had lingered in her heart they had now fled.

The pain was raw but she welcomed it. It gave her the strength to turn and look at him then for the first time with eyes that held no echoes of the past, no secret hopes for the future, just the cold reality of the present.

'It doesn't matter, Cal,' she said quietly. 'It really doesn't matter at all.'

CHAPTER SIX

'It's good to have you back, Claire. We've missed you. This valentine promotion of yours has really taken off!'

'I'm glad to hear it, Tom. I'd better get down to work, then, hadn't I? Maybe I'll see you later.'

'Of course. You can give me a run-down on what happened in New York.' He walked away but not before Claire had seen the fleeting disappointment on his face at her rather obvious dismissal. She sighed, wondering if she should call him back, but what was the point of doing that? She would never feel anything more for Tom than friendship. Michael Callan had ruined her chances of falling in love with anyone else.

The morning was hectic. With only two days left before St Valentine's Day, Claire had lost count of the number of cards she'd sold. She should have felt proud that the promotion was such a huge success but it was hard to feel anything apart from this icy numbness that had filled her ever since that night at the penthouse. She'd not spoken to Cal since, not that she'd wanted to. He had said all that needed to be said then.

When lunchtime came she carried on working, only stopping late in the afternoon to make a cup of coffee in the office. Wearily she closed the door on the throng of shoppers and picked up the kettle, then stopped abruptly when she saw the sheaf of roses lying on her desk. For a moment she stood and stared at them in surprise, then she put the kettle down and picked them up, searching through the wrapping paper for a card to say who had sent them, but there was nothing apart from a slip of paper with her name on it stapled to the Cellophane. They were beautiful, deep red and velvety, their perfume filling the air, but who could have sent them? Unless. . .

She dialled Tom's office, her voice warm when he answered. 'It's Claire. I just wanted to say thank you. They're gorgeous.'

There was a moment's silence then Tom spoke. 'Sorry, but I've no idea what you are talking about, Claire.'

'You mean you didn't send me the roses?' Her bewilderment was obvious and he laughed with a trace of embarrassment.

'I'm afraid not. I wish I had done, though. It was a nice way to welcome you back.'

'Oh, I see. Sorry. I expect I shall find out who they *are* from soon enough.' She replaced the receiver and stared at the flowers as though they could supply the answer to the mystery, but it eluded her for the rest of the day.

The following morning it was violets, a huge, hand-painted china bowl of them standing on the filing cabinet. Claire slowly closed the door and walked over to touch a gentle finger to the velvety petals. Once again there was no card, just a slip of paper bearing her name taped to the bowl. She stood in silence then reached for the phone before abruptly putting it down again. Was it wise to phone Tom and thank him again for something he might not have sent? Logically, they must be from him, prompted by guilt after yesterday, but she didn't want to make any more embarrassing mistakes.

When the box appeared on her desk the next day she'd just got back from lunch. Tom had made no mention of the violets and short of asking him outright she'd been unable to get to the bottom of the mystery. Now as she spotted the gaily wrapped parcel she felt her stomach churn. Slowly she closed the door and walked across the room but it was several minutes before she could make herself unwrap the parcel, and she gasped in astonishment at what she found inside.

Sugar mice, a dozen of them, perfectly sculpted in pink and white, nestling in a bed of crackling black paper inside a silver-filigree box that bore the now familiar slip of paper with her name printed on it. What on earth was going on? Was it some sort of a joke? Because if it was she failed to see the funny side of it!

The questions whirled around her head all afternoon long until she felt quite dizzy with them, her whole body consumed with tension, her nerves quite raw. When the message came for her to go up to the office just as she was ready to leave that evening, it seemed like the final straw. All she wanted was to get home to the quiet safety of her flat and think through what had happened, find some sort of sensible answer to it all. This delay seemed almost more than she could bear. She marched upstairs and into the office after only the most cursory of knocks, then stopped dead when she found it empty.

For a moment she stood irresolutely then turned to leave, feeling her heart pounding sickeningly when she suddenly spotted the envelope propped up on the desk with her name printed on it. Tension hummed along her veins and she clenched her hands into fists, staring almost wildly at the plain white envelope, knowing that there was no power on earth that would make her pick it up and see what it contained.

'Why don't you open it, Claire?'

His voice was deep and quiet in the silence. It filled her head and sent quaking shudders racing through her body. She pressed a fist to her lips and closed her eyes, praying that her imagination was playing tricks, but when he spoke again she knew it had been no mistake.

'Open it, Claire. Go on.'

She shook her head, her face as white as the envelope, her eyes huge and haunted. 'No.'

He smiled gently, drawing her gaze as he moved across the room from where he'd been standing in the shadows by the window and picked up the envelope and held it out to her. 'Trust me, Claire. Open it.'

'Trust you?' The pain was stark and unadorned as it echoed in her voice. She made no attempt to hide it, nor did she try to disguise the contempt that was shimmering in her eyes as she stared back at him. 'I would sooner trust a rattlesnake than trust you, Michael Callan!'

Red ran along his cheekbones in a thin, angry line but his gaze was level, his voice steady. 'I know I've hurt you, Claire, but I am asking you to give me one last chance, and I promise that I won't ever hurt you again.'

'Why should I? Why should I give you anything? Frankly, Cal, you've had all I'm prepared to give. . .ever!' She pushed past him, wanting only to get out of the room and away from this fresh nightmare, but he caught her arm and stopped her, swinging her round to face him so that she was forced to look straight into his eyes.

'Why, Claire? Because you love me.' His voice was deep, filled with something that seemed to cut straight through to her heart. Just for a moment Claire allowed herself to imagine that he meant what those soft, seductive tones implied, then deliberately pushed such foolish ideas from her head.

'Yes, I love you. But that doesn't mean that I'm willing to let you walk all over me again! You made it very clear what you wanted from me in New York, Cal, so don't insult me now by pretending anything else. I know exactly where I stand with you now, and what I feel for you has no bearing whatsoever on our business dealings!'

'And you really think that you can separate your emotions into neat little compartments like that?' There was disbelief in the question and she glared at him, more hurt that he should do this to her than she could admit.

'Yes! You do it all the time, so why should it be so different for me?' She laughed harshly, tossing her head so that her hair swirled back from her face. 'You are a true master of your emotions, Cal. You can turn them on and off at will, and I've used you as a role model!'

He sighed, his eyes sweeping over her face with gentle patience before he reached out to smooth a stray wisp of hair back from her cheek. 'I thought I could control my emotions, Claire, but that was before you came back into my life. 'You've always been my Achilles' heel.' He picked up the envelope and ripped it open, smiling in a way that made her heart thunder as he held her gaze and spoke softly, words that seemed to make no sense at first. '"Roses are red, violets are blue, sugar is sweet, and. . ." Well, I think this says it all for me.'

He held the card out to her, but Claire made no attempt to take it. She couldn't. She felt as though she'd just been pole-axed. Red roses, blue violets, sugar mice. . .

'It was you? You sent all those things!'

He laughed deeply, taking her hands to draw her to him. 'Yes, and you need one last very important item to complete the list. Here you are, Claire. Won't you take it?'

He handed her the card, his eyes filled with an expression that made her feel hot and dizzy and breathless all at the same time. Claire stared down at the card, her hands shaking so much that she could barely open it, and read the message written beneath the red satin heart.

'I do, Claire. I love you. I've written it there and I'm telling you it now. I love you with all my heart and all I want is to hear if you love me, as I hope and pray that you still do.'

'I. . .I. . . Oh, Cal!' The card fell from her hands as she hurled herself into his arms, burying her face into the curve of his neck as she held him close. He closed his eyes, a deep shudder running through him as his arms tightened around her.

'Thank God! I've been so afraid that I'd destroyed everything you felt for me. I don't deserve you to love me, Claire.'

There was anguish in his deep voice and she looked

up, smoothing a hand lovingly down his cheek, trembling when he turned his head and pressed his lips to her palm. 'It isn't that easy to destroy love, Cal.' She laughed almost sadly. 'Although I must confess that I tried to do it many times during these past years, and tried even harder since that night in New York. But you're in my heart, in my blood, in my soul. If I destroyed what I feel for you then I would be destroying part of myself as well.'

He bent and kissed her fiercely, his mouth possessive as it took hers in a kiss of naked passion. 'I can't make up for what I've done but I shall try, Claire. I shall try my hardest!'

She shook her head, glorying in the feel of his lips on hers, the sheer possessiveness of his hold. 'The past is over and done with, Cal. Let's not dwell on it.' She stopped uncertainly, her eyes clouding. 'You're sure that you mean what you say? I don't think I could bear to go through another break-up.'

'I'm sure. I've never been more certain of anything in my life. I knew that night in the lift how I really felt about you, and it shook me!'

She laughed at the wry admission, moving closer as she slid her arms around him under the soft folds of his jacket. 'Is that why you acted so coldly afterwards? Because you didn't want to face up to how you felt?'

'Yes, dammit! It was madness, Claire, but such delicious madness. It's haunted my dreams, I can tell you, remembering how you looked standing there in that lift!'

She laughed shakily, her blood heating at the note of desire in his voice. 'And that's when you finally realised you still loved me?'

'No. That's when I finally *admitted* it.' He tilted her face up to his, his expression very grave. 'I have always loved you, Claire. I never stopped loving you. I just tried to bury it at the back of my mind because I couldn't afford such feelings.'

'I wish you'd told me, Cal. I wish you'd explained instead of leaving with barely a word spoken.' She looked away, not wanting to mar this sudden gift of happiness yet all too aware that it wasn't easy to ignore the past. 'You couldn't have loved me that much, I don't think.'

He framed her face with his hands. 'I did. I ended our relationship because I had no choice but to do so.' He let her go and walked over to the window, his face etched with pain. Claire wanted to run to him and hold him, tell him that it didn't matter, but in her heart she knew it must all be sorted out before they could think about the future.

'Why not?' she asked quietly. 'Why didn't you tell me who you really were right from the beginning, Cal?'

'Because I'd promised my uncle that I wouldn't say anything to anyone at the store. The plan was that I would gain some much needed practical experience before moving into a management position.' He shrugged. 'I'd never been interested in working in the family business, if you want the truth, but felt beholden to after my parents were killed. My mother was a Hadley before her marriage and it's through her that I inherited my stock in the company. When my uncle suggested that I should take an interest in it I agreed mainly because I knew that was what she would have wanted. However, I never imagined that I would be thrust in at the deep end so quickly.'

He ran a hand almost wearily through his hair, his eyes softening as they went back to her. 'Has anyone ever told you how beautiful you are, Miss Parkinson?'

Her blood ran thick and she shivered delicately, feeling the look like a caress. 'Hundreds!' She smiled as his face darkened. 'But never anyone who mattered. . . apart from you.'

He smiled arrogantly, not missing the slight huskiness in her voice. 'Good. But before I get side-tracked I had better finish my story, hadn't I?'

'Only if you want to tell me, Cal,' she said softly, her eyes adoring him openly.

'I do. I want this out of the way now, Claire. It's way past time I explained anyway.' He seemed to gather himself, then continued firmly, as though he had thought often about what he would say. 'I wanted to tell you the truth about who I was many times, even discussed it with my uncle, but although he left the final decision up to me I never did it, and then it was too late.'

'Why? Did you think it would make a difference, Cal?'

He shrugged. 'Maybe. I liked what we had, Claire. I valued it. I didn't want it to change. I'd had experience of how attitudes change in direct response to the amount of money a person has and I didn't want that to happen with us.'

Her eyes flashed and she stared back at him hotly. 'I don't give a damn how much money you have or haven't got, Michael Callan! That doesn't influence my feelings one iota!'

'I know, I know. But it might have put a constraint on our relationship and that was something I wasn't willing to risk. Also there was the very real chance that other people would find out who I was once I started telling the truth, and that was something I didn't want to happen. I needed to learn the business from the ground up, not be treated differently because I was one of the Hadley family.'

'I suppose I can understand that.'

'I hope you can, Claire.' He smiled lovingly at her. 'It's very important to me that you try to understand how I felt and why I acted the way I did.

'Well, things were going along quite well until fate took a hand in it all. My uncle had his first heart attack and found that he couldn't keep the control he should over the business. There was an attempted take-over at the American end which would have meant the breakdown of the whole chain. Uncle John was too sick to fly over and sort it out so it was suddenly down to me. I had just two days to get things under control again and convince the shareholders that Hadley's was still a good investment. That's why I left so abruptly.'

'But you could have explained that to me, Cal!'

He shook his head, his face set and uncompromising. 'I didn't have enough time, Claire. It was touch-and-go as to whether I could get the support I needed to retain control.'

'I could have gone with you, helped you in any way I could!'

'No one could help me. It was down to me, the whole future of Hadley's. I worked twenty-hour days for that first year and not much less after that. I knew it would be hard. I knew that I wouldn't have time for a personal life, Claire. The business had to come first and foremost if it was to survive. It wasn't fair to as you to go with me then desert you. It would have ended in bitterness and heartache and I couldn't do that to you because I care too much. I convinced myself that it was better to make the break swift than let what we had die a painful death.' He shrugged. 'Perhaps I was wrong but I don't think so. I still believe that it was the only thing to do in the circumstances.'

Was he right? Would the pressure have been too great for them to have sustained their relationship? With the hindsight of maturity, Claire could see that it might have been. She had grown up a lot these past three years, changed from a girl into a woman. That made a world of difference to her outlook.

Suddenly the pain that had lain in her heart for so long faded, leaving her filled with joy. Cal hadn't left her because he no longer cared about her, but because he had cared too much!

She went to him, slipping her hands into his in a gesture of trust that made him draw in a slow, deep breath as his fingers tightened around hers. 'I love you,' she said softly. 'I never stopped loving you and I never shall.'

He pulled her to him, holding her so close that she could feel his heart thundering against the swell of her breast. 'My God, Claire, but you can't have any idea how I've longed to hear you say that! I thought I'd ruined everything, but thank heavens I haven't!' He smoothed kisses across her eyelids, her cheeks, fleeting tokens of love and tenderness that made her ache. 'I knew I still felt attracted to you as soon as I saw you again but you seemed so determined to keep our dealings on a business footing.' His eyes gleamed wickedly as he brushed her mouth with his then drew back tormentingly with a seductive smile that seemed to melt her backbone so that she had to cling to him. 'And *that* made me determined to alter things. But it was only after what happened in the lift that I faced the fact I was still in love with you, that it wasn't just desire I felt.'

Claire pressed against him, loving the feel of his body hard and taut against hers. 'So what happens now?'

'Oh, that's up to you.'

'Me? What do you mean?' She drew back a fraction, confusion on her face as she stared up at him.

'Well, I've been the one making all the proposals of late, so now I think it's your turn.'

'Proposals?' She sounded like a parrot, repeating every word, but it was hard to follow what he meant.

'Yes, proposals. I mean, you do want to make an honest man of me, Claire, don't you? After almost compromising me in that lift?'

'Me compromise you? Huh! And as for making an honest man of you, I've no idea what you...' She stopped short, suddenly realising what he was saying. 'This isn't...isn't leap year, Cal,' she whispered huskily.

'I won't tell if you won't.' He feathered a kiss across her parted lips, drawing tantalisingly away just out of reach when she started to respond.

'Cal!' Frustration echoed in the sound of his name and he smiled tormentingly as he ran a finger across the soft, ripe fullness of her lower lip, teasing the warm flesh until she gave a little moan, part-protest, part-desire.

'You know the answer, Claire. You want me, don't

you, my sweet? But I am a man of principles. I need to know that this is going to be a permanent commitment.'

'I. . .' Desire was making her dizzy and she closed her eyes then opened them again slowly to look up into his handsome face. She loved him so much; to think of having the right to love him for the rest of her life suddenly gave her courage.

'I love you, Cal. Will you marry me?'

His whole body stilled then abruptly his mouth came down and he kissed her hard before he drew back to look straight into her eyes. 'Yes. I love you too, Claire, probably more than you can ever imagine. Now let's get out of here!'

He started across the room, taking her with him, making her breathless with his haste. Claire laughed, pulling back to make him slow down.

'Hey, stop a minute. What's the rush?'

He turned and caught both her hands in his, raising them to his lips to kiss them. 'The rush is because I can't wait a minute longer than strictly necessary to make love to you.'

'Oh!'

'Oh, indeed.' He laughed as he ran a finger along the soft flush of colour that stained her cheeks then led her out of the office and into the lift, taking her into his arms as soon as the doors had closed. His kiss was hot and tender, demanding and giving, everything she'd ever longed for and dreamt about. It seemed to draw the very essence from her, wrapping her deep in its magical spell so that it was several minutes before she realised that the lift had stopped.

She drew back, staring round in confusion. 'We seem to have stopped again.'

'There's no "seem" about it.' He held up the key he had taken from the control panel then slipped it into his pocket and let the jacket drop to the floor. 'This time, Claire, I'm taking no chances on being interrupted, so if you have any objections then voice them now.'

She smiled seductively, her hands going to the buttons on her blouse, her eyes loving him as she worked them loose. 'I've no objections, Cal. After all, this is St Valentine's Day, the one day in the year just meant for lovers!' And stepped back into his arms.

Modern Romance™
...seduction and passion guaranteed

Tender Romance™
...love affairs that last a lifetime

Sensual Romance™
...sassy, sexy and seductive

Blaze™
...sultry days and steamy nights

Medical Romance™
...medical drama on the pulse

Historical Romance™
...rich, vivid and passionate

29 new titles every month.

With all kinds of Romance for every kind of mood...

MILLS & BOON®

Makes any time special™

MAT4

Tender Romance™
6 brand new titles each month
...love affairs
that last a lifetime
Available on subscription every month
from the Reader Service™
GEN/02/RS2

Modern Romance™
8 brand new titles each month
...seduction and passion guaranteed
Available on subscription every month from the Reader Service™
GEN/01/RS2

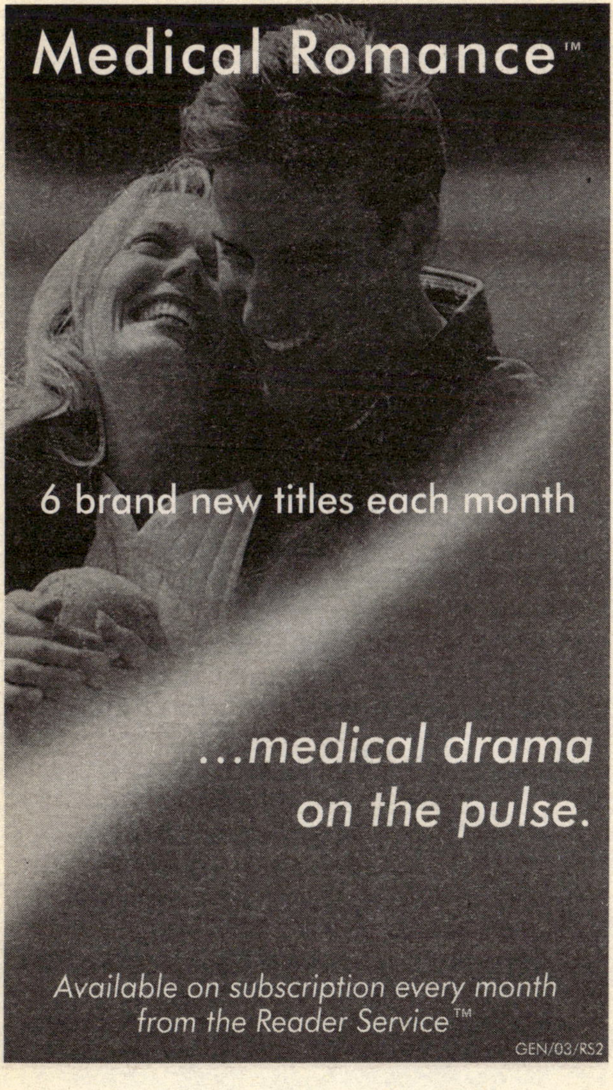
Medical Romance™
6 brand new titles each month
...medical drama
on the pulse.
Available on subscription every month
from the Reader Service™
GEN/03/RS2

Historical Romance™
4 brand new titles each month
...rich, vivid
and passionate
Available on subscription every month
from the Reader Service™
GEN/04/RS2

Sensual Romance™
4 brand new titles each month
...sassy, sexy
and seductive.
Available on subscription every month
from the Reader Service™
GEN/21/RS2